'Mrs Kelly's having contractions, Leigh.'

'What!' he exclaimed.

'Contractions!' She was laughing now. 'Do you realise that we're stuck out here, hundreds of miles from hospital and help, no one even knowing we're here, with a pregnant woman with a broken arm who's having contractions at thirty-three weeks, a senile old man, and four children. Doesn't it almost strike you as rather funny?'

She went on laughing as the sound of the plane faded in the sky, and then there were tears too, cascading down her sun-pinkened cheeks, and sobs high in her throat that mixed with the laughter and made her shoulders shake.

'Stop, Nerida!' ordered Leigh. 'Just stop!'

But she couldn't, she was helpless, and a moment later he took a long step towards her and hit her full on one cheek, a stinging slap with the flat of his hand . . .

Lilian Darcy lives in Sydney, Australia. As well as romances she also writes for the theatre, films and television, and her interests include winter sports, music and French. She says she writes Doctor-Nurse Romances because it gives her the opportunity to create heroines who are real, who work for their living, care about what they do and lead interesting and fulfilling lives. Although she has no medical training she has many friends in the profession who delight in providing her with details. They have even been known to get into heated arguments over the exact treatment her hero ought to prescribe!

CALLING AIR DOCTOR THREE

BY

LILIAN DARCY

MILLS & BOON LIMITED
ETON HOUSE 18–24 PARADISE ROAD
RICHMOND SURREY TW9 1SR

First published in Great Britain 1988
by Mills & Boon Limited

© Lilian Darcy 1988

Australian copyright 1988
Philippine copyright 1988

ISBN 0 263 76078 2

Set in 10 on 10½ pt Linotron Times
03–0588–60,050

Photoset by Rowland Phototypesetting Limited
Bury St Edmunds, Suffolk
Made and printed in Great Britain by
William Collins Sons & Co. Limited, Glasgow

CHAPTER ONE

'BUT it's a marvellous opportunity!' Mrs Reid expostulated, not troubling to conceal her impatience.

She sat back in her chair, fixing Nerida Palmer with an irritated stare. A shaft of warm Sydney sunlight caught at her aggressively copper-coloured hair and outlined the thin metal frames of her businesslike glasses. Difficult to believe that this was July, the middle of the Australian winter.

'Yes, I know,' replied Nerida, firmly but a little hesitantly. 'But I don't feel that I'm the right person for the job. Of course everyone has heard of the Royal Flying Doctor Service . . . I'm sure it's very exciting and adventurous, but I know nothing about outback life. I'm from London. I've never even . . .'

'Yes, all right, if you feel that way then there's no more to be said. I'll have to find someone else.' Mrs Reid was already reaching for her files, her long, brightly-painted nails clicking together as she rustled the papers. 'However, I'm afraid I have nothing else to offer you at the moment.'

'Oh.'

'I thought you'd jump at this. I really can't understand you . . . but never mind.'

'Yes, sorry . . .' muttered Nerida.

'Perhaps if you could ring in, in a couple of weeks. Or I may contact you if something comes up.' Mrs Reid's tone announced this to be an unlikely possibility.

'Thank you.' Nerida rose to depart, recognising the words as a dismissal.

As she passed through the reception area, Julia Crowe, the secretary at Reid's, gave her a sympathetic smile. 'Poor Hilary's under a lot of strain at home,' she mouthed. 'She and her husband have just split up, and she's a bit frantic. Don't take any notice.'

Nerida nodded in sudden comprehension, but out in the cool stairwell, she had to pause to collect herself as she shrugged her shoulders into the lightweight grey wool coat which was all that was needed for outdoor winter warmth in this climate. She hadn't enjoyed one moment of that interview.

Reid's was a good nursing agency, with a well-earned reputation for arranging short-term placements at very short notice. Nerida was very pleased to be on their books, but encounters with Mrs Reid herself—always frighteningly snappy and brisk, and always armed with the absolute conviction that her arrangements were perfect for all parties concerned—were never an enjoyable experience, and today's had been easily the worst. It was understandable, after what Julia Crowe had just said, but was not pleasant all the same.

Up until now, Nerida had been happy with her placements. There had been one or two stints of relief work in the familiar atmosphere of a large hospital, and several varied and interesting interludes with private patients or in smaller convalescent hospitals. Having come to Australia for a year's working holiday in March, Nerida felt that she had expanded her horizons, had some worthwhile experiences and met some interesting people so far, all in atmospheres of relative safety.

Coming to Australia in the first place was adventurous enough, since she had known no one here, she considered. You could push yourself into challenges that were *too* great, then collapse under the strain, and what was the point of that? What had you proved? What good had you done for anybody else?

Which was why she had engendered Mrs Reid's profound irritation by turning down that 'marvellous opportunity' with the Royal Flying Doctor Service. Nerida knew her own limitations—or thought she did. She was a city girl. She felt this quite definitely as she tapped down the single flight of stairs in her modest-heeled shoes and stepped into the busy, noisy street. It would be naïve and dangerous to think that she could slip into the role of nurse with the Flying Doctor Service and do a good job in conditions that were so utterly foreign to her, amongst people whose whole way of life was an unknown quantity.

It sounded well enough in fantasy—the adventure of a lifetime, something every other nurse of her acquaintance would envy—but the reality . . . Nerida felt that it would be fair neither to herself, the Service, nor the patients to inflict herself upon them.

She sighed, nonetheless, as she stood at the bus stop. Mrs Reid had said to 'ring in a couple of weeks.' What was she to do in the meantime? Travel about a bit? But she didn't have all that much money; this was a working holiday. Or she could see a bit more of Sydney. It was a beautiful city, but being a tourist alone . . . It would be fun, but somehow not quite what she felt like.

Back home, Nerida made herself a cup of coffee and a snack, and curled up in a big armchair with some travel pamphlets. It was still only late morning.

She was lucky to have found this house—or rather, household. It was a small terrace in the suburb of Balmain, with the harbour all around and some lovely waterfront parks nearby. Two Australian nurses had advertised for a 'third girl to share', and the three of them did get on well. Susie and Genevieve had their own lives, though—busy work schedules, a range of leisure activities, steady boyfriends—and Nerida had to battle with loneliness at times. Still, that was silly. She was very glad to be here in the stimulation of a new environment, instead of . . .

For the first time in weeks she thought of Damon. He had been, literally, the boy next door, all through her teens in London. They had started going out together after she left school, and had become engaged when she was in her third year of nursing.

'We'll have to wait, of course,' he had said earnestly at

the time. 'Till I finish my course.' He was an engineering student at Farnborough.

'We can wait,' Nerida had said earnestly in reply.

It had been rather hard at first, but then she had got into the habit of going out with nursing friends. They had a lot of fun, and the fact that she only saw Damon at weekends or days off seemed to matter surprisingly little. She was happy, of course, and in love, but somehow love was rather a confining thing and made you want to sit at home and watch television a lot, absently holding hands, rather than going out and taking up new interests.

It had come as sheer unadulterated and blissful relief one day when Damon had sheepishly announced that he had 'fallen for' another girl and wanted to break off their engagement. Nerida had been completely appalled at herself. Had she really felt that fettered and bored without even realising it? Did she understand so little about the workings of her own heart?

The whole drawn-out affair seemed to have left no impression at all on her inner self, either. What had she learnt about life from their time together? What challenges had their relationship put before her? But the departure of Damon certainly signalled one thing: the need for change.

'I must find out who I am and what I want,' she thought wildly one day as she found herself reaching for his ring to twist in a gesture that had unconsciously been habitual. First, as usual, came the shock—'It's not there!' Then, also as usual, the sweet flood of thankfulness—'I'm free!'

But for what? Nursing? She loved it, of course. She liked activity, and to keep her hands and mind busy. She enjoyed the varied contact with people and she even liked the routine. It wasn't enough to fill a whole life, though.

In the Damon era—that was how she thought of it now—she had vaguely assumed that domestic matters would provide that 'other dimension' one day. But now she wanted to question all that. If she had been so bored and imprisoned merely being engaged to Damon, how would she have felt as his wife?

Surely courtship and marriage should be exciting, and difficult, too, at times! That was what had been wrong between her and Damon; it had all been too placid and easy. She could scarcely remember a time when they hadn't known each other. Never had there been a sense of discovery, of wonder and excitement and adventure.

'I must *do* something!' Again the wild thought had come to her. And again, 'But what?'

The answer had presented itself a few days later, quite surprisingly and unexpectedly, in the form of a suggestion from a nursing friend that they go to Australia for a year on a working holiday. It was surprising because Nerida and Rosemary weren't particularly close friends; however, they got on well enough, and plans were almost finalised when Rosemary announced that she was pulling out. She had met a wonderful man and . . . well, they were engaged. Rather ironic, really, when you thought about it.

For a day or two Nerida was depressed and adrift, and then, quite suddenly, it didn't matter a bit. After all, she and Rosemary *weren't* close friends, so there was no element of personal hurt at being let down. She would go to Australia by herself.

So she did, and here she was, several months later, and homesickness was the kind of emotion that could lead to another bout of interminable and mindless television watching. It was time to take herself firmly in hand. Perhaps a trip up the North Coast would be nice.

The phone rang, breaking her reverie.

'Hullo, Miss Palmer? Hilary Reid here.'

'Yes, this is Miss Palmer.' Nerida raked back her dark curls with a slim hand and made a face at the electric wall clock. Had something come up after all?

'There's no one else on our books at present who is available for the Flying Doctor placement.' The crisp tones came clearly through the line. Nerida could hear the controlled tension and anguish now, though, after what Mrs Reid's secretary had said, and had to feel sympathy, in spite of the fact that she couldn't like the woman all that much. 'I would very much appreciate it if you would reconsider your decision.'

'I see . . .' Nerida said doubtfully.

'It *is* urgent. Sister Walters has had to fly off to Brisbane to be with her mother—I told you her father had died suddenly, didn't I?—so they're at present without a nurse altogether. Surely out of human compassion you can respond to . . .'

'Yes, all right, of course.' For once it was Nerida who had interrupted her employer.

Reading between the lines, she knew that Mrs Reid was more concerned with the reputation of her agency than with the plight of the Service, and that 'I would very much appreciate it if you would . . .' really meant 'You will no longer be on our books if you don't . . .' But it was the first reason that convinced her. If the situation was urgent, then she felt she had to put aside her own qualms and hope that the outback community would do the same.

She'd probably have to leave tomorrow morning. Perhaps she would be able to go to the local library this afternoon and find a book on the Flying Doctor Service, so that at least they would not find her utterly ignorant about its history and way of operating.

'When will I have to go up there?' she asked.

'I've arranged for you to pick up your ticket at the airline counter. Your flight to Broken Hill leaves at two.'

'This afternoon?' It was already a quarter past twelve. Half an hour check-in time, half an hour in the taxi . . .

'Yes. If you hadn't let me down this morning you might have been halfway there by now. I hope that won't have set you off on a bad footing with Benanda Base.'

'How do I get from Broken Hill to Benanda?' This must be only one of a dozen questions Nerida needed to ask, but she couldn't think of any of the others.

'There's a mining company plane going up to the gasfields. They'll drop you off on their way through.'

A vision of herself plummeting from the cargo hold of the plane along with a couple of mailbags presented itself to Nerida's dazed mind.

'I see.' Most of her clothes were still damp on the clothesline in the backyard, she had precisely three dollars and fifty-two cents in her purse, so she'd have to get to the bank, lunch would be out of the question, but no doubt they'd serve something on the flight . . .

'Good. I'm glad that's all settled,' said Mrs Reid. 'Thank you for being so willing.'

'But what do I . . . ? Do I have to . . . ?' Nerida paused. She didn't really know what was asking.

'Yes?'

'It doesn't matter.'

'Well, goodbye then, and good luck,' said Hilary Reid. 'Oh, by the way, take a raincoat. They've been having a bit of wet weather, I hear. And let me know how it goes.'

For a minute Nerida stood with the receiver held rather limply in one hand, then she remembered that she had precisely three-quarters of an hour in which to tidy up her life and pack it in a suitcase—at which point she realised she had absolutely no idea of how long she would even *be* in Benanda, so it was about time she got going.

Damp washing in plastic bags, dry washing kept separate, an impatient wait in the lunchtime queue at the bank, a note to her housemates. Should she ring for a taxi or walk up to the main street? She should have gone to the bank on her way to the taxi rank . . . And which airline counter was holding her ticket? At least three companies flew the Broken Hill route . . .

It seemed like a miracle to Nerida that she managed to get on the plane at all. But she did—it was the second airline she tried—and here she was, at last able to catch her breath.

The city shrank rapidly below, a wayward pattern of

square red roofs, oval blue swimming pools, flat green parks, grey streets, higgledy-piggledy factories, cars crawling like ants. Then in no time they had left the urban landscape behind, and Australia's narrow coastal belt of vegetation and population gave way to the sparse heartlands where rust-coloured earth stretched for miles and miles, broken up only by irregularly-scoured hills and rock formations, winding sandy rivers lined with dusty gums, clusters of farm buildings, tanks, windmills, stockyards and herds.

It was surprisingly green, though, in parts, and most of the rivers seemed to be flowing. Mrs Reid had mentioned wet weather; that was good. The place wouldn't be too desert-like, and it wasn't summer, so Nerida wouldn't risk the ignominy of wilting under unaccustomed heat.

'Landing soon, by the feel of the plane.' The middle-aged businessman seated next to her spoke laconically, taking her by surprise. So far he had only smiled once and then lowered his balding head over the papers spread in front of his less-than-flat stomach.

'Yes, the time's gone quickly,' Nerida nodded. 'It's been so interesting to look at the landscape.'

'Not been up this way before?'

'No,' she replied, adding, 'I'm English.'

'Could tell that. What, on holidays, are you?'

'Sort of. A working holiday.'

'Nice,' he nodded. 'Hope you like it up here. Stopping at the Hill?'

'Sorry, I . . .' she began.

'My fault. Broken Hill, I mean. Locals call it the Hill.'

'No, I'm going up to a place called Benanda. There's a Flying Doctor base there, and I'll be working as a nurse.'

Her new acquaintance whistled through his teeth at this piece of information, and looked at her for a second or two with narrowed eyes, but didn't offer any further comment. It was a slightly unsettling reaction as far as Nerida was concerned. Could he tell just from her appearance and their brief snatch of conversation that she'd be an utter failure at the job? A fish out of water? Dangerously ignorant about the environment in which she was to work? But he was speaking again.

'Lots of single men up there. Pretty girl like you. Don't get yourself into any trouble.'

'I certainly don't intend to,' replied Nerida, a little coolly. There had been an innuendo in his words that she didn't like. Perhaps it was fortunate that the flight was about to end.

Nerida *was* pretty, but her awareness of this fact had not given her a swelled head, or otherwise altered her personality. She was slim, not tall but not tiny either, with a head of lustrous golden hair that sat in lively natural waves. Her eyes were dark and her skin pale and fine, with just the tiniest dappling of freckles after a dose of summer sun. Her nose was straight, but would wrinkle up in a gamine fashion when she smiled her open white-teethed smile, and her lips were evenly moulded above a small but quite firm chin.

Prettiness does not simply consist of colouring and features, however, and Nerida's attractive appearance was as much the result of quietly confident posture and bearing, a lively way of moving head and hands, and a general friendliness towards the world, as of long-lashed eyes and a graceful profile.

However, she had never thought of her looks as something that might 'get her into trouble' with a lot of 'single men', and she didn't want to start thinking like that now, when there was so much else about the world she would soon be entering that was potentially challenging and difficult.

Suddenly she felt her stomach drop away and her throat tighten, and it wasn't because the plane was about to land. Things had happened so fast since this morning that she hadn't had time to think, but now all her earlier qualms were returning, and all at once she had an overwhelming longing not to be here at all. Not even to be in Sydney, but to be *home* in London where there were parents, a beloved younger sister, old friends, and above all routine—dull, too familiar, but *safe*!

An hour later, she had not entirely succeeded in shaking off this mood, and the flight from Broken Hill to Benanda wasn't helping. The small company plane was full, taking workers at the Tanama gasfields back to their jobs after holidays spent down south. It was all too evident that most of them were the single men she had been warned of by her acquaintance on the Broken Hill plane.

Many were nice, and others might have been if they had not been affected by peer-group mentality, but some were downright unpleasant. Whether it was the tail end of holiday exuberance, or the release of frustration at having to return to work, or whether, in a few cases, it was simply the result of having too much to drink in the Broken Hill airport bar, some of the men were being loud and obnoxious and crude, and much of their banter was directed at Nerida herself.

'Nurse, eh? Wouldn't mind *you* giving me a blanket bath!' This came from a particularly unattractive specimen, red-faced and overweight and raucous of voice, whose mates addressed him as Gobbo.

'Here, Nurse, I'm in a fever, I want me temperature taken.' This from an older sharp-featured foreman.

'I can't breathe, I want mouth-to-mouth resuscitation.' Gobbo again.

'And then another beer!' A third grinning fellow.

'Leave her alone! Can't ya see she's tired, ya drongoes!' The very Australian epithet brought a faint smile to Nerida's lips, though she concealed it by turning her head to the window. The speaker came from the much quieter group at the front of the plane, where Nerida wished with all her heart that she was sitting.

'Shii-ugar! There go my bloody ears popping!' another man exclaimed, which meant, thank heavens, that the flight would soon be over. It was late afternoon, and it had seemed like a very long and bewildering day.

It was cool and windy on the airstrip, and the place seemed very bare. Dappled grey cloud blanketed the sky high up—they had been flying above it since just before Broken Hill. Nerida found that here in the open she was not quite warmly enough dressed. So they did have winter in the desert! She stood by the plane, feeling her hair tangling around her ears and neck as a crewman from the gasfields plane quickly unloaded her baggage.

'Not too heavy for you, is it, love?' he asked with genial haste.

The plane's engines kept up their low whine and Nerida could smell the blast of acrid exhaust fumes. Clearly no one wanted to wait while her luggage was transported into that low building nearby—if that was where she was supposed to go. She assumed it must be, since there didn't appear to be any other place in the vicinity. Presumably the plane was supposed to be back at Tanama before nightfall, and this unscheduled detour was slowing them down.

'No, I can manage,' Nerida said to the crewman.

'Sure?'

'Quite sure.'

'See ya later, then.'

'Yes, goodbye, and thank you.'

Why would he see her later? Perhaps people ran into each other frequently in the outback. Or perhaps it was simply a standard Australian expression of farewell.

Even as she picked up her suitcase and swung the strap of her bag on to her shoulder, the plane was taxiing slowly out to its take-off position. An extra bit of breeze plucked at the hem of her dark textured wool skirt and opened the lapels of her jacket to chill her skin beneath the thin silver-blue blouse she wore. Repressing a shiver and stifling her mounting sense of isolation, Nerida began to walk towards the sprawling building.

At that moment a tall figure appeared at a doorway in the distance. It seemed to take a long time to cover the wide expanse of bare red ground between them. At first, she expected the man to come forward to meet her, but instead he simply stood impassively—watching her, she guessed, although she could not yet see his face clearly.

Then, just as a set of regular features, dark slate-brown hair and steady eyes were beginning to resolve above white denim jeans and a blue shirt, just as Nerida was about to smile a greeting, he disappeared inside the building again.

'Rude!' she thought. 'Or is it just because I'm tired that it seems that way?'

No, it *was* rude. He hadn't come forward to help with her luggage—which was growing heavier by the minute —and he hadn't even waved or called hullo. What kind of a reception was that, when she had come all this way at such short notice?

Then, just as she was having to blink back tears of annoyance and homesickness, he appeared again, quite close by this time. Now she could see that the steady eyes were a cool, piercing and intelligent blue, that the slate-brown hair was a little untidy, and that the face was that of a man in his early thirties, relatively unlined and yet containing something that hinted at tension and strain.

'Glad to see you made it at last. Let me take that.' He held his hand out for her suitcase, and Nerida handed it over. Another casual outback greeting, it seemed. 'You're Miss Palmer. Nerida . . . have I said that right? Accent on the first syllable?'

'Yes, that's right.'

'You're English.' He had picked her accent after three words.

'Yes,' she said again. 'I'm out here on a working holiday.'

He said nothing further and turned away, but not before Nerida had caught a glimpse of the transformation in his face. His welcome, terse and abstracted though it was, had at least contained the suggestion of friendliness, but that had dropped from his expression altogether, to be replaced by an unreadable set of jaw and furrow of brow.

As she followed him inside, wincing a little when she accidentally let the screen door bang behind her, Nerida again felt a mixture of anger and homesickness rising inside her. A strange town, a demanding job, and this as a welcome!

'Would you like tea?' he asked.

'Yes, please, that would be lovely.'

Free now to look around her, Nerida saw that she had entered a pleasantly bright, cream-painted kitchen area that faced towards the airstrip and was complete with sink, small stove and fridge. The dark-haired man, well-built and ruggedly tanned, who had not, she realised, condescended to introduce himself, was pouring water from an electric kettle into a glossy brown china tea-pot.

Two white cups sat ready in their saucers, beside a plate of home-made 'Anzac' biscuits. No refreshments had been offered on the flight to Benanda, and Nerida had felt too churned up by her whirlwind departure to eat a proper lunch on the flight to Broken Hill. Now she realised that she was both hungry and thirsty, and the idea of a cup of tea appealed enormously.

'That looks good,' she said impulsively, feeling that she, at least, might as well try to be friendly.

'That's right, you English are so fond of your tea, aren't you?' her companion said.

Actually, in fact, Nerida generally preferred coffee, and resented the man's easy categorisation of her tastes, but she shut her white teeth together firmly and said nothing about it. You couldn't quarrel with a man who was probably going to be your boss—especially when you didn't even know his name. *Temporary* boss, she reminded herself. It was an unlucky thought.

'How long do I have to stay here?' she blurted, without stopping to consider the wisdom of the question.

'Stay here?' He paused in his action of pouring the tea,

and his eyes lifted slowly to hers.

'Yes, at Benanda. Mrs Reid didn't say.'

'You've only just arrived. Have you decided you don't like it already?' There was controlled anger in the question. Nerida sensed it and let her own emotions rise to the surface.

'Well, you haven't made me very welcome,' she retorted.

'I've made you a cup of tea.' The dry humour was a surprise, but Nerida did not allow it to deflect her.

'I don't even know your name, but I presume . . .'

'Dr Russell—Leigh Russell. You haven't bothered to find out very much, have you?'

'I've scarcely had time, Dr Russell!'

'And neither have I. Do you have any idea what conditions are like up here at the moment? No, of course you don't! You're fresh out from England . . .'

'I've been in Australia since March.'

He ignored this completely. '. . . And you mess us all around, changing your mind, changing your flight . . . What do you know of life out here?'

'Not much, and that's why . . .'

'Mrs Reid said on Monday that she was sending a thoroughly competent and experienced nurse, and now, after two days of phone calls and arrangements, I get a fresh-faced English rose, who . . .'

'Listen, Dr Russell!' Nerida burst out. 'I didn't want this job. I didn't want to come all the way out here.'

'Then why on earth did you?'

'I did it out of a sense of duty because I was told it was an emergency. And now I find I'm not wanted at all.'

'Oh, you're wanted all right. You were wanted two days ago.'

'Two days ago? I was told at twelve-fifteen this afternoon, and my plane left at two!'

There was a sudden silence, a moment frozen in time. Nerida's gaze was locked with that of her new adversary, and she found time to wonder what on earth two strangers were doing arguing like this. It was ridiculous and degrading, and it had all got out of control far too quickly.

'There's obviously been some mistake.' Leigh Russell broke the silence, speaking crisply still, but with less anger. He added milk to one cup of tea, and hovered questioningly over the other.

'Yes, please,' Nerida said quickly. 'No sugar.'

'I rang Reid's first thing Monday morning and was told that Mrs Reid had just the right person, and that she'd ring back to confirm flight details. I heard nothing. I rang on Tuesday and found that she was out of the office, and Mrs Crowe knew nothing about the matter as Mrs Reid had been dealing with it all herself.' He was speaking with studied patience. 'I rang this morning and was told it was all under control. The girl had pulled out but was now willing again, and would be on the plane at eleven. Finally at lunchtime, I was informed that you'd be catching the three o'clock plane to Broken Hill, and I'd have to arrange transport up from there.'

'There's been a mistake, then,' Nerida nodded.

She could make a hazy guess at what had happened. Due to Mrs Reid's crisis at home, her usual well-oiled mechanisms had gone awry. She had forgotten to telephone, or she had found that someone who was listed as available was in fact *not*, and, rather than jeopardise the reputation of Reid's, she had put the confusion down to Nerida's 'change of mind'.

Would Nerida say all this to Dr Russell, or would it sound like tale-telling? Taking her first sip of tea, she pondered the question. She would have to say something, so that the terrible footing they had begun on did not continue.

'Leigh!' An older man entered the kitchen from the open corridor that adjoined it. 'Emergency radio call from Kilalpanundra.'

A second later both men had disappeared, and then Nerida heard a third male voice, accompanied by heavy footsteps, and the crash of a screen door. She sipped her tea numbly. Was the new arrival headed this way? And if so, what would *he* have to say to her? Would he be as dangerous and unpleasant a specimen as Dr Leigh Russell? Yes, here he was.

'Hullo, you're the new nurse,' he greeted her.

'Yes.'

'I'm Jim Stenning, I pilot Air Doctor Three. Pleased to meet you.'

'My name's Nerida—Nerida Palmer. And I'm pleased to meet you too.'

She *was* pleased, very definitely. A friendly face at last! In his middle thirties, she guessed, short and stocky, with green eyes and a rather overgrown reddish moustache.

'We've had a bit of trouble getting you up here, apparently,' Jim went on.

'Yes, it's been a bit hectic and difficult for me too,' Nerida smiled.

'Has it? I was off duty or flying with Ralph Stevens all yesterday and today. Leigh's been handling it all. It's come at a bad time. Poor Jenny, her dad's death was very sudden and it's knocked her mother out completely.'

'Yes . . . I'm still very unclear about it all.' Nerida furrowed her smooth brow for a moment and took some more tea. Jim Stenning seemed very willing to talk, so perhaps at last she could get rid of this awful feeling of having no idea what was going on, that had only been compounded by that nasty flare-up between herself and Dr Russell. 'How long . . . is she expected to be away?'

'We don't know. Leigh didn't want to ask her to be too definite. Her mum hasn't got much support in Brisbane, so she might not come back at all. She's going to let us know in a couple of days if we'll be looking for a permanent replacement.'

'And how long would that take to arrange?'

'Depends,' he replied vaguely, then grinned. 'Any more tea going?'

'I think so.' Nerida gestured at the pot, and he looked inside, then got out a cup.

Not as helpful as Nerida had hoped. She still didn't know whether to expect to be here for days or for weeks.

Rain clattered suddenly on the roof of the building, and on looking out, she found that the sky had lowered. Darkness was gathering as the sun set, and the clouds stretched the colour of shadowy steel as far as she could see.

'The forecast's bad.' Brisk footsteps accompanied the words and announced Leigh's return. He was followed closely by the older man, who Nerida guessed must be the Base's radio operator. 'Setting in for days in the north-east, apparently, though most of our region to the west should clear tomorrow. But it's the last thing we need, what with the flood-waters from the eastern rivers peaking all through here pretty soon.'

'You don't have to tell me,' the radio operator said.

'But we have to take my old girl up now, right?' Jim Stenning put in, laying down his tea cup with a reluctant grimace.

'Right,' nodded Leigh Russell. 'Stockman fallen badly from his horse at Kilalpanundra. Their strip's pretty dry and they can rig up lights, which is good. This rain hasn't got there yet. We'll need . . .'

He looked across at Nerida and she could see his hesitation. Unconsciously she allowed her face to express what she felt: sheer dread. Hadn't today been long and unsettling enough already? Did she really have to start work straight away? She would, of course, if necessary, but . . .

'No, we won't take you, don't worry,' Leigh Russell responded to her unworded thoughts, and she flushed at the hard vein of sarcasm in his tone. He thought she was weak, and a coward. Was he right? She raised her head in sudden pride, and the flush became out of determination.

'Of course I'll come,' she told him.

'You won't,' he said firmly. 'It's not necessary. Better to get settled in at Mrs Hammond's—you're boarding there. From tomorrow onwards the work'll be pretty heavy. We're evacuating.'

'Evacuating?' She could only echo the word stupidly.

'The floods.' He saw that her expression was still blank. 'Don't you read the papers?'

'Yes, but . . .'

'Explain to her, Martin, would you? Jim and I have to get going.'

He snatched a coat off a peg behind the door, picked up a bag of equipment and headed out into the dark rain, closely followed by Jim Stenning. Nerida got to her feet, her legs feeling like cotton wool, and went to the sink to wash the cups. There were a number of dirty ones already there. She had lost any chance to explain to Dr Russell about the mix-up at Reid's. If she brought it up at a later date, it would only seem like a manufactured excuse, and now he already had enough reasons to think badly of her.

The fresh dampness of rain came through the open window, as well as the sound of two voices.

'. . . pretty.' She only caught this last word of Jim's comment, but Leigh Russell's reply came clearly just before they strode out of earshot:

'Pretty useless!'

Nerida bit her lip. Martin was still standing there. He had heard it too, she knew. If she pretended that she *hadn't*, would he ingore the comment?

'Don't worry about the cups,' he said. 'You must be tired. I'll drop you at Mrs Hammond's.'

'It'll only take a minute.' She was determined to prove herself at something, even if it was only washing cups. And even though Dr Russell wasn't there to see.

'Things are a bit tough here at the moment,' said Martin, picking up a tea-towel. 'Bit of bad luck for your first day. You see, we've got rivers rising all through the Benanda Base sector. All the rain that fell in the catchment areas to the north and east of here is heading downstream towards Lake Eyre, and we've had local downpours as well. Like this lot now.'

He gestured out of the window. It was coming down even heavier now. The doctor and his pilot had already disappeared, and Nerida caught the sound of an aeroplane engine roaring into life, above the sound of the torrent.

'Leigh's been busting his guts trying to co-ordinate things with the local emergency and disaster service, but he and Brigadier Harris—ex-Army man, a real pain in the . . . Anyway, they rub each other up the wrong way. He's having a rotten time. But it's supposedly pretty well organised now.'

'And that's what's happening tomorrow?' Nerida questioned a little stiffly. Her father was an ex-Army brigadier, and she loved him dearly.

'Yes. The Brigadier's crew are handling general evacuations, herding of stock to higher ground, feed drops and all that, but anyone who's at risk medically is being flown out of flood-affected areas by our planes. And there's the regular medical work to do too, so you'll be making a lot of stops. It'll be a long few days, specially if this lot keeps up.' He gestured into the darkness again.

It looked menacing and desolate. They finished the cups in silence, and Nerida heard the plane passing overhead as it gained height. She imagined Leigh Russell strapped moodily into his seat, his body tense and his face set in the frown he had already flung several times at her.

Martin seemed to blame Brigadier Harris for the fact that the two men did not get on, but Nerida was convinced that the fault must be on both sides. If Dr Russell went round delivering those menacing looks and terse criticisms to everyone, it was surprising he had any supporters at all, not to speak of friends.

She wondered suddenly if he was married. Some women would certainly find him physically attractive, with those steady blue eyes, that well-built torso and those firm, cynical lips. *She* didn't, of course. If she didn't like a man's character, she couldn't like his looks.

'Well then, let's pick up that suitcase and head off to Mrs Hammond's, shall we?' Martin said.

CHAPTER TWO

NERIDA couldn't sleep—ludicrous and annoying after her long day. She rolled over inside a hot twist of sheets and blankets for what must be the twentieth time, to look at the luminous green hands of the little travelling alarm clock that she had managed to remember to bring.

A quarter past three, and she felt she'd scarcely closed her eyes. The rain falling on the metal roof ought to have been a soothing sound, but it wasn't, because it only reminded her of the fact that at six—less than three hours away—she was to be collected in Leigh Russell's car and delivered to the waiting plane so that they could embark on the increasingly urgent evacuation work.

Nerida rolled over again. The unfamiliar room, although pleasant and cosy, was full of shadowy shapes, unexplained creaks, and the scent of rose-flavoured cleaning products.

'I'm like a cat, I like my own place and my own scents,' she thought.

And yet she had had a pleasant evening. Lorna Hammond had accommodated Benanda Base's nurses for several years in the caretaker's flat of a planned-for but never built motel at the back of her petrol station, providing them with an evening meal and leaving breakfast and lunch up to them. She was friendly and energetic in typical outback fashion, and was a mine of information about the history of the town and the operation of the Royal Flying Doctor Service.

Nerida found out that this base had been going for only a little over four years, and that the small hospital in the town was even newer. Benanda was expanding in its quiet way. A national park had recently been created in some interesting hill country to the north-east, and further mining exploration was taking place nearby.

The town was not losing its outback character, though. The annual picnic races were still a major event, local young people would still travel hundreds of miles to attend 'Bachelors' and Spinsters' Balls' in larger towns further south, and it was still possible to wander down the middle of the main street at most hours of the day without much risk of being run over.

Nerida and Mrs Hammond had sat talking for quite a long time over their evening meal of sausages, chips and vegetables, followed by several cups of tea.

'I'm going to have to change my drinking habits,' Nerida had realised.

And at the end of the session she had felt that she understood much more about what lay ahead.

But now it was all buzzing around inside her brain, and she simply could not switch it off. In two hours the tinny rattle of the alarm would sound, she'd have to make breakfast in the kitchen-cum-lounge of the caretaker's flat from the provisions Jenny Walters had left, and dress in the uniform that Martin Baird had rummaged up for her from a cupboard at the Base building. Then Leigh Russell would appear. Not a relaxing thought.

At that point Nerida gave up on sleep, switched on the bedside lamp, and reached for the paperback novel she had begun on the plane. A few minutes later it had slipped from her limp fingers and at last she slept.

There was a very irritating banging going on. It would stop for a few seconds and then start again. Someone was calling out something too, in a loud, impatient half-whisper.

'Miss Palmer! For heaven's sake—Nerida Palmer!' It was her own name.

Suddenly, appalled wakefulness flooded her. That was Leigh Russell's voice. Her bedside light was still on, and the alarm read six. It hadn't gone off. A quick check revealed that she had not set it properly.

'Yes, I'm awake,' she managed to call. 'I'm sorry . . . the alarm . . .'

This was too terrible! Only a few hours' sleep and she had to face the justifiable annoyance of that terrible man again. She hurried to the door, aware that her floral cotton nightdress was rather thin, and she had brought no dressing-gown. But she couldn't leave him standing out there in the still-dripping rain. She opened the door and there he stood, the shoulders of the khaki shirt he wore already damp, and a mist of moist droplets covering his hair. His eyes flicked briefly over her scanty attire, then moved away as if he couldn't care less what she was or wasn't wearing.

'Come in,' Nerida said ineffectually.

It was still dark outside. The rain had lessened noticeably, but the day looked gloomy all the same. Leigh Russell came in, saying nothing but looking volumes. Nerida did not waste any more time on explanations or apologies about the alarm, but disappeared immediately into the bathroom. She'd had a shower last night, so a splash would have to do this morning. Breakfast, of course, was out of the question.

In a few minutes she was able to survey herself in the mirror and feel satisfied. Simple white dress topped with navy blue cardigan, rather thick, practical cinnamon-coloured tights and flat white leather shoes, hair brushed into a fluffy set of fair waves, and that would have to do. She could hear Leigh Russell moving about in the room and wondered what he was doing. It was sheer impatient pacing, probably.

'Ready!' She hoped it sounded efficient, and that she'd been quick enough to please him—if it was ever possible to actually *please* this man, she amended, catching his impassive expression full in the face yet again.

He said nothing, but swept her up and down with his cold blue gaze, and then, in a couple of strides, had moved through the small lounge and into the adjoining bedroom. She followed him. What on earth was this about? He was opening the wardrobe door and a couple of the drawers in the small chest that sat next to it, and flinging out several items—her raincoat, a pair of jeans, a blouse, a fluffy salmon-pink pullover, socks, and even her sponge-bag from the bathroom.

'I'm sorry, I thought the uniform . . .' she began.

'Yes, but you might need a change of clothing. Did you bring an overnight bag?'

'No, I didn't realise . . .'

'You may not need all this, but it's best to be on the safe side.'

There was a large plastic carry-bag on top of the wardrobe, that bore the name of a fashionable chain of women's clothing shops. Obviously it belonged to Jenny Walters. It felt strange to be amongst her things, although she and Mrs Hammond had managed to pack most of them away. Leigh Russell reached for the bag and slid the garments and sponge-bag inside.

Nerida held out her hand to take it from him, but he shook his head as he led the way back into the little lounge and kitchen.

'You'll need both hands to eat breakfast,' he told her.

It was only then that she noticed what he had done while she had been in the bathroom. A tall glass of orange juice stood on the laminex bench, and beside it were two pieces of toast, one spread thickly with marma-lade, and the other spread thinly with Vegemite, a peculiar Australian substance—yeast extract, Nerida believed—for which she was only just beginning to acquire a slight tolerance. Still, with the long day ahead, and goodness knew what chance of eating later on, she would have to force it down.

'You'll be eating as we drive, so no time for a hot drink, I'm afraid,' said Leigh.

'No, of course not. Thank you for this.'

'You'll need it.'

She picked up the orange juice and gulped it quickly, then balanced a piece of toast in each hand and pushed open the screen door with one elbow. Leigh Russell followed, locking the main door and letting the screen door flap gently to close.

His four-wheel-drive vehicle was parked directly outside and she scrambled awkwardly into it after he had opened the door for her. He waited patiently, then shut it and walked round to the driver's side with measured stride, narrowing his eyes and glancing up at the sky, which was beginning to lighten now to a watery grey. It was a far cry from the glowing red dawns of the travel brochures.

Nerida wondered what he was thinking, and whether he was always this taciturn. Her own feelings were a mixture of acute embarrassment and consciousness of her own ineptness, and anger at the fact that he seemed to be going out of his way to make the whole situation worse. Didn't he realise that if only he was a little warmer, a little more polite and friendly, she wouldn't feel so ham-fisted, so helpless and miserably ignorant?

Oh, she disliked him intensely! Why on earth was she here putting herself through this? She had only come out of duty and compassion, out of a belief that it was urgent, and he didn't even want her, had not expressed one shred of gratitude.

It took only a few minutes to reach the Base. Already the simple layout of the little town was becoming familiar. One wide main street, with a narrow strip of bitumen in the centre, contained almost all of Benanda's houses and public buildings. There was a church with attached community hall, a small school, and opposite the Base itself, the cool modern building that was the new hospital.

Leigh Russell did not point any of this out, however. It had been Martin who had explained it all the night before.

Signs of life were starting up in a few of the houses. There was a light or two in kitchens at the back of houses and of the hotel, and a rooster and a dog heralded the morning from their large, untidy yards. In its way, Benanda did not look like a bad place.

Nerida finished her first piece of toast as Leigh swung the wheel impatiently to turn into the small car-park beside the Base.

'I've got some things to collect,' he said. 'You go straight to the plane.'

He noticed that she had a free hand again and swung the plastic bag of clothing towards her. She caught at it clumsily. Couldn't he do anything politely?

It wasn't raining as she walked to the plane, but the air was damp and it was quite chilly. The navy cardigan and cotton uniform weren't really enough. Still, once the sun rose the air would get warmer, and no doubt the aircraft itself would be a comfortable temperature.

It was an Australian-made Nomad, painted with the emblem and colours of the Royal Flying Doctor Service —a twin-engined, propeller-driven machine, Martin had explained yesterday. Not that this meant much to Nerida. The engines were already running, Jim Stenning was in the pilot seat, and the door was open. The climb up inside was a little awkward; Nerida felt the skirt of her uniform strain across her legs and a gust of wind whip around her knees. The toast and marmalade had to be balanced very carefully, but then she was inside and safely seated.

'Morning, Nerida,' Jim said cheerfully. First names were evidently the order of the day in this environment.

'Morning,' she replied, trying to give it the same jaunty inflection that he had used, but not quite succeeding. She had so little idea of what lay ahead!

She saw Leigh Russell striding out to the plane, carrying a couple of medical bags. His face still looked grim. She thought back on their two encounters. Had she seen him smile even once? Not that she could remember. Martin Baird would put it down to the contretemps with Brigadier Harris over evacuation procedures, no doubt, but Nerida wasn't inclined to be so forgiving. She felt quite sure that the fault must lie with Dr Russell himself.

As if to confirm this opinion, Leigh Russell began to speak about the Brigadier as soon as he had got into the plane and swung himself into the seat at Jim Stenning's side. The man's name was pronounced with a

whipcrack of irritation, above the rising whine of the
engines.

'Harris rang, would you believe? While I was collect-
ing the gear.'

'Oh yes?' Jim said mildly, concentrating on his equipment. He did flash a quick sidelong glance at Leigh
Russell, however.

'We're not to go to Tingaringi, although it was agreed
yesterday that it was to be our first port of call. He says
the whole family is going out by four-wheel-drive—on
his advice. I hope to high heaven they get through. Mrs
Stockton is far from strong enough . . .'

He clamped his mouth shut over the last words,
spoken through gritted teeth, as if his anger would not
let him go on. There was a brief crackling silence as Jim
manoeuvred the aircraft to the end of the airstrip ready
for take-off, then Leigh Russell broke into speech
again.

'I'm talking about human lives, and Harris is fiddling
around with . . .'

'Economical resource deployment,' Jim finished for
him.

There was a sudden throaty bark of laughter from the
angry doctor, which made Nerida start in her seat and
lock her tense muscles even tighter. It wasn't laughter
that relaxed the atmosphere, although it did reveal a
further glimpse of the man's sardonic humour that she
had noticed yesterday.

'That's exactly it,' said Leigh Russell. 'It's funny
—and yet it's not.'

He lapsed into silence again, staring out of the window
at the sparsely vegetated landscape under its canopy of
soft pearl-grey cloud. Nerida did the same as she finished
her second piece of toast.

She was still battling with an intense longing to be
almost anywhere but here—home in London for preference. This was all so very unfamiliar. A plane trip
signalled a holiday, not the start of days of hectic and
important work. She knew there were questions she

should be asking, but did not trust herself to ask the right ones, and in his present mood she could see that Leigh Russell would not suffer a fool gladly. Better to sit in silence.

The small plane gathered speed along the runway, and with a final gentle bump left the earth to gain height rapidly before wheeling around to the west. The landscape, for a few moments, was like a wall map tilted crazily to one side, and Nerida saw for the first time exactly what the floods meant.

Rivers and creeks were swollen, trees that normally stood well up the bank were a-swirl with muddy waters, and water lay in ditches all along roads and farm tracks. In one place she saw that a river had broken its banks completely and spread into a series of braided streams, rejoining and parting again, draining off into shallow ponds, flowing slowly but unstoppably towards the huge salt lake hundreds of miles away, which was journey's end.

It was fascinating and terrible to see nature's power and whim at work like this, but then the view was blocked, first by torn shreds of grey mist, then by the thick low cloud, and a few minutes later they had emerged above it into the fathomless blue sky.

Nerida turned away from the window and found herself idly studying Leigh Russell instead. He had a map spread out before him, and a sheet of paper with a list of names.

'Perhaps we should head for Patamunda first, in that case,' he was saying.

'Yes, that'd be sensible,' Jim Stenning nodded. 'What's happening there?'

'Jock O'Loughlin's staying, with two of his stockmen. They've got most of the cattle on to high ground where there's some feed. They've got to try and herd the rest through a bit of water to get them safe. They reckon they'll be able to see it through till the flood-peak passes. Their road out is OK. Annie and the children will go with the other stockman by four-wheel-drive. It should be fine.' He spoke in measured tones. His voice was actually quite well timbred, pleasant on the ear, when it wasn't tightened by anger.

'So why are we stopping?' asked Jim.

'Jock gashed his leg open yesterday and wants to make sure it'll be all right,' replied Leigh. 'He won't exactly be working in hygienic conditions. And the toddler's been a bit sickly. Annie is wondering if we should take him back to Benanda in the plane and he'll stay with her sister there.'

'Fair enough,' Jim nodded, then silence fell again.

Leigh's hands rested on the crackly surface of the map and he stared ahead. He hadn't spoken to her once since he had got into the plane, Nerida realised. Jim had thrown her a casual grin once he had steadied the plane on its course, and the engine whine made the cabin too noisy for real conversation, but she felt isolated, alone and unwanted, nonetheless.

After her sleepless night she couldn't help brooding over it, and couldn't summon a determination to keep a stiff upper lip. To her horror she knew that she was going to cry, and felt the first sob tighten in her throat and tears course down her cheeks. For several minutes she simply gave way to the feeling, resting her head against the moulded plastic edge of the window and almost enjoying the luxury of self-pity. If only she were home safe in England! She was normally a strong-willed, bright-natured person, but wouldn't anyone wilt under these circumstances?

Perhaps not! The thought struck suddenly. I'm here now. Shouldn't I try to make the best of it? Leigh Russell's a complete horror, but Jim Stenning's not too bad, and Mrs Hammond.

Surreptitiously, Nerida got out a handkerchief to dry her eyes, and froze momentarily as she became aware that Dr Russell's cool blue regard was fixed in her direction. How long had he been watching her? She set her jaw firmly and calmly brought the white handkerchief to her face and nose, still returning his gaze. She would brazen this out. What business was it of his if she *was* crying?

'Homesick?' The laconic question came out quietly and not urgently. Caught off guard, Nerida could only nod. 'You'll get over it,' he said lightly, and turned away again.

So that was his idea of sympathy, was it? She was fuming now. He must really detest her, really have a low opinion of her, and what right did he have? What justification? He knew nothing about her, and hadn't even tried to find out. She would soon prove him wrong. She might know nothing about outback life, she might not have lived through a natural disaster like this before, but she was a very well trained nurse, and Dr Russell was going to know about it! She would grit her teeth and carry on, even if she turned out to be operating on cattle!

Aggressively she wiped one final time at red eyes and moist nose, then put her handkerchief away and sat up very straight. Leigh Russell turned around again.

'We'll be landing fairly soon,' he explained above the noise of the aircraft. 'I'd better fill you in on a few things.'

'Yes, that'd be good,' Nerida nodded firmly.

She noticed a fleeting glint of . . . could it be satisfaction? . . . in the rugged man's startling sapphire eyes, and a suspicion flashed over her. Had he intended to provoke this reaction of anger and firmness in her? Surely not! He didn't know her at all. How could he have guessed the way her feelings worked?

She leaned forward in her seat in order to hear him better, and to study the map over which his surprisingly muscular though smooth and fine-boned hands were hovering.

'These are the places we hope to get to today,' he began. 'See, the floodwaters are moving down through here, swollen by local rains in some parts, although this lot should be clearing soon, according to the forecast . . .'

Twenty minutes later, with Nerida feeling slightly

more in the picture, they were on the ground at Pata-munda. It had stopped raining for the time being, but pale cloud still hung overhead, and the temperature outside was cool. Nerida put on her forest green raincoat as a protection against the damp, fresh wind, and stood on the muddy red ground of the airstrip, watching as a rather battered Land Rover came lumbering towards them.

'Jock's at the wheel, so his leg can't be too bad,' said Jim.

'Jock O'Loughlin could drive that vehicle with no legs at all, if he had to,' Leigh responded drily.

As if to confirm this opinion, Jock lowered himself gingerly from the driver's seat, wincing as he did so, and Nerida caught her breath at the sight of a long welt of new blood rapidly staining his work-worn beige trousers.

'Jock . . .' said Leigh, gesturing at the place after handshakes had been exchanged.

'Eh?' Jock O'Loughlin glanced down and saw the red patch. 'Damn! Must have split it again in the boat.'

'What boat?' Nerida wondered to herself. Then she saw that Jock was looking at her. She smiled, and he grinned back.

'You heard about Jenny's dad?' Leigh Russell asked.

'Yeah, poor girl,' Jock nodded.

'This is our temporary replacement.' Was there an extra stress on the word 'temporary'? 'Nerida Palmer.'

'Nice to meet you, Nerida,' the bluff, cheerful man nodded. He had a leathery face and hands, and a maze of wrinkles from squinting too much in the sun, but Nerida guessed that beneath his battered hat there would be reddish hair, not grey, and that in fact he would only be about forty.

'Take the front seat, Nerida,' said Leigh, his blue eyes direct and cool. 'It'll be a rough ride.'

Pointless to protest that a rough ride wouldn't kill her. Nerida decided to save herself for later more significant chances to prove her worth, although she could tell that

Leigh Russell was waiting for a fresh sign of weakness in her.

It *was* a rough ride, and slippery too. Jock swore under his breath several times as the vehicle slithered dangerously close to the water-filled ditches at the side of the track, or bounced through a pothole whose depth had been concealed by its muddy surface.

But it was when they arrived at the belt of graceful, white-trunked gums that marked the creek that Nerida had to bite her lip to keep from exclaiming aloud. How on earth were they going to cross that fast-flowing tea-coloured torrent? It was at least a hundred yards wide, and Jock was heading straight for it. Nerida could see the homestead now, several hundred yards beyond the far bank, a shrub-surrounded sprawl of buildings on a rise that would remain just out of reach of these record flood-waters.

Just as Nerida was on the verge of panic—did Jock expect this machine to *fly* across that sheet of water? —he wheeled around and came to a skidded stop beneath a tree, within feet of the water's edge. Only then did Nerida notice the open aluminium dinghy with small outboard motor attached, and on the other side of the creek, another Land Rover. They were making this journey in three stages.

She hid her fear as they approached the small— awfully small!—craft. The blood was seeping in a widening circle across Jock O'Loughlin's thigh. She saw Leigh glance at it, frowning, then met his gaze herself.

'He knows I'm frightened, but he'll never get me to admit it!' she thought.

'Can stay behind if you like,' Jim volunteered in his laconic way. He had mentally put four adult bodies into that boat as Nerida had, and seen that it would be a tight fit.

'No, come across and have a cup of tea with the missus,' urged Jock. 'The current's not as bad as it looks.'

'Oh, good,' muttered Nerida darkly. Jim gave a shout

of laughter, having caught the aside, and even Leigh chuckled briefly. He didn't say anything, however.

'You first, Nerida,' said Jock.

'OK,' she replied gamely, her voice a little thin, and clambered awkwardly up to the bows.

Jim came next, carrying the medical equipment, and Leigh stood back to help Jock in. It was evident that his leg was giving him more pain than he was happy about. He sat down heavily, making the craft lurch as Leigh pushed it off the mud bank and leapt into it across the widening space of water.

For a moment everything rocked dangerously, and Jock gave a groan of pain as he knocked the wound on the hard metal of the boat's edge. He clutched his leg, releasing the rudder, and they began to drift downstream more and more rapidly as the current caught at the dinghy and pulled it further out from the bank. In a second Leigh had grabbed at the rudder.

'The motor's idling, how do I get it into gear?' he asked.

'Black lever to the left, there,' Jock managed to say. Nerida's heart was in her mouth. There were snags in these flooded rivers—fallen logs concealed beneath the tea-coloured waters that could hole a boat or overturn it . . .

'Got it!' said Leigh, his voice steady but his teeth clenched.

For a moment or two their direction was still uncertain. Leigh tried to correct their course too quickly and a dangerous wall of water pushed up one side of the dinghy, but then at last they were heading smoothly for the far bank, and after all it wasn't a long journey. In no time they had slid up the muddy slope and Jock was laughing heartily.

'All in a day's work, eh, Doc?'

'You're going to need a good few stitches in that leg, Jock, and that'll be work,' Leigh replied.

'I'll drive this bit, shall I?' offered Jim, and Jock nodded. 'Then we'll all have had a go.'

'Except me,' Nerida pointed out, deadpan. 'Perhaps I'll have to tackle the return trip.'

She was rewarded by laughter, even from Leigh Russell, and surprisingly she found herself smiling back at him, her lips parted and her straight nose wrinkled a little.

Annie O'Loughlin had come out to meet them when they arrived at the homestead. She was carrying a red-faced crying little boy of about two, who did not look very healthy. Nerida remembered Leigh's comments about him on the plane.

'The kids are inside doing School of the Air lessons,' she said to Leigh after greeting everyone briefly and being introduced to Nerida. 'We'll be leaving as soon as you've advised me about Sam and looked at Jock's leg.'

'We'll be doing more than look at it, Annie,' Leigh told her. 'Look at his trousers.'

She did so, and exclaimed roundly, 'Jock, you crazy man! I told you to be careful!'

'I was,' he said, not put out. 'Don't know how it happened. Hit it again coming back in the boat too. There's too much to do, that's the trouble. I can't keep my mind on it.'

'Well, Dr Russell'll keep your mind on it,' his wife retorted cheerfully. 'I bet he's planning to put in heaps of stitches and it'll hurt like hell.'

'I'll give him a local anaesthetic,' said Leigh.

'Serve him right if you didn't,' retorted Annie. Her tongue was sharp, but there was humour and acceptance in everything she said, and Nerida quite enjoyed it. Perhaps this was the attitude to cultivate if you wanted to live in the outback. 'I'll put on some tea, shall I?'

'We can't stay too long,' Jim put in. 'Got a long day still ahead.'

'Just a quick one, while we decide about Sammy here.'

They all trooped into the house, with Nerida's heart lifting a little at last. She felt happier than she had done since ages ago when she had first found out that she was to come up here. Ages ago? It had been *yesterday*!

She found herself in a large living area, in one corner of which sat three children, two girls and a boy, aged between nine and five. They were intent on lessons, communicating with their teacher hundreds of miles away via two-way radio, but they glanced up, smiled and said hullo when they saw the new arrivals.

Nerida wondered if all outback children were as disciplined about their lessons. She guessed that Annie O'Loughlin had a lot to do with it. She was a woman who would run her family firmly, but with an encouraging twinkle in her eye the whole time.

'Now, let's have a look at that leg,' Leigh said with authority, as Annie went to put on the kettle.

Jock led the way into the main bedroom, wincing at each step now that his absorption in the journey from the airstrip to the homestead was over. Leigh carried the bag of equipment, which he proceeded to open straight away. Nerida suddenly felt the most ludicrous fondness for some of the items he brought out. This was nursing! This was something she knew about, even if she had never nursed in conditions like these before.

Gingerly Jock removed his blood-soaked trousers. Nerida spread a plastic sheet and a towel across the bed and he lay down on it while Leigh carefully unwrapped the bandage from the work-hardened thigh.

It was quite a competent dressing, she noticed. Leigh had explained on the plane this morning that each outback homestead had a special well-stocked medical chest, containing standardised numbered items. Mrs O'Loughlin had also done a good first-aid course, so she had been able to treat and dress the wound very well, following instructions radioed through yesterday afternoon by Ralph Stevens, Benanda Base's junior doctor.

'When did you last have a tetanus booster?' Leigh was asking. Jock narrowed his eyes in an effort to remember, then the doctor continued.

'We can radio Benanda and get it looked up in your file. I should have remembered to check that myself before we came, but I've had so much else to think of.'

'No, it's OK. About two years ago, it was—two and a half, in Clifford Ransome's time. I remember it because it was Janet Ransome's first clinic flight. Janet Green, she was then, of course.' He chuckled as he thought back on what had evidently been a medical romance of much local interest, then winced and caught his breath as Leigh Russell's sensitive fingers probed the wound gently.

'No foreign matter in there, anyway. And that booster should still be effective—Annie's done a good job. But we'll need to stitch it up. That extra split you gave it this morning has done some damage. Nerida, would you prepare an anaesthetic?'

He named an amount and Nerida got the syringe ready, then swabbed the area with disinfectant. Jock made no sound as Leigh guided the needle in cleanly, but one hand twitched, and Nerida knew it would have hurt. She prepared sutures and had other instruments at the ready, then stood waiting while the edges of the wound were neatly sewn together. Finally she applied a new dressing as Leigh packed away the rest of the equipment and spoke earnestly with Jock.

'Sam's eczema hasn't improved with the new treatment?'

'Not really. Annie's really worried. And he seems to have a bit of a temperature at the moment, too. I wondered if he'd got something else. Andy Gangali's kids have had measles. Our lot got immunised a few years ago, I remember, and of course Sam wasn't born then. But the eczema . . . I don't know.'

'The water out here wouldn't help,' Leigh said thoughtfully. 'Your tanks are pretty old, aren't they?'

'Yeah.'

'We might look at that. A new tank, with a special lining. But of course that's in the long term. Right now we have to decide if he goes by road with Annie, or flies with us.'

'Could you take him, Doc?' asked Jock. 'I know you're stretched at the moment, but Annie's more worried than she lets on. The other three just grew up like weeds, healthy as anything, no problems at all, but little Sammy's different.'

'Of course we'll take him,' Leigh reassured the worried father, who got up and limped out of the room, a grin of relief spreading over his sun-lined face, both at the decision about Sam and at the fact that the messy business of his leg was over and done with.

'We'll leave him some changes of dressing and some antiseptic powder, I suppose?' queried Nerida, hovering over the equipment.

'Yes, they'll have those things in their kit, but we'll leave extra. Jock and Bill and Andy will be camped out with their stock until the flood-peak passes, heaven help them, so we'll have to give him strict instructions about keeping it clean,' Leigh replied absently, frowning. 'Getting enough water will be a problem.'

'It will?' Nerida couldn't believe this. To her, it seemed as if there was water everywhere.

'Drinking water, I mean,' Leigh explained. 'Clean water. Where they're camped a lot of the water will have been lying round too long. It'll be stagnant, brackish. Or it'll have had stock moving through it, animals dying in it . . .'

'Of course, yes, I hadn't thought,' Nerida murmured.

'Hadn't you?' His brow cleared and he seemed only then to become properly aware of her standing there gazing at him intently with her dark eyes as she absorbed all this new information. 'No, I don't suppose you had.'

She could see him taking stock of her slim build, her delicate English skin, the tense, expectant pose she had unconsciously adopted as if she was waiting for some new surprise or danger to hit her from any direction at any time . . . His features tightened in irritation once more.

'We can't just stand here. We've got to drink that tea and then get going. We're behind schedule already.' He was walking to the door as he spoke, having swung the medical bag into one hand. Then he turned back. 'But actually, you did a good job just then.'

There was something in the tone and wording that Nerida resented, and she let it show.

'Well, I am trained,' she said bitingly. 'Did you doubt even that?'

He smiled faintly at this, but did not venture a reply and was out of the room ahead of her a moment later. Nerida fumed impotently, and could only follow him.

CHAPTER THREE

THE PLANE droned on, lulling Nerida into a near-doze. Little Sam O'Loughlin was asleep, mercifully, cuddled in her lap with one small dry hand clutching the corner of her cardigan. He had cried from the moment Annie had relinquished him at the passenger door of the Land Rover to the time when, fifteen minutes after take-off, the smooth flight and Nerida's warm lap and soothing words had at last quietened him.

The journey back to the airstrip had been hair-raising again, but somehow the little child who had been put into Nerida's charge had called forth deeper resources within her. It was his safety that was her greatest concern, and she had simply sat through it, after taking a few deep breaths, and was surprised at how little fear and discomfort she had felt.

Mrs O'Loughlin was planning to begin the long drive to greater safety and support straight away. She would have the three older children and a junior stockman for company, while Jock and the other two stockmen, Andy and Big Bill, would make their way upstream in the motor dinghy, with supplies and cattle dogs towed behind in a smaller rubber launch, to where the stock were herded on higher ground. There they would sit out the flood-peak, overseeing aircraft drops of feed if they became necessary, and keeping the herd from panicking and from straying into dangerous areas.

All this was no longer Nerida's concern. The child stirred in her lap, his poor little face and hands scaly from eczema and his forehead flushed from fever. It seemed all too likely that he had caught measles from the head stockman's children, but by late this afternoon he would be safe in Benanda, where his Aunt Kath would

43

provide loving care, and where he could be hospitalised if necessary'.

Nerida's ears cleared suddenly, after feeling like cotton wool for some time without her being consciously aware of it, and she realised that the aircraft had begun its descent to Coolamon Creek.

'No river crossings this time, you'll be pleased to hear, Nerida,' Jim called back to her, then his attention was caught by a heavy sigh from Leigh Russell as he glanced at his watch. 'We can only do what we can do, Doc, eh?'

'I know.'

'So save your strength for facing Harris again on Monday for the next co-ordination meeting.'

Leigh only nodded in reply, closing his startling eyes for a moment as he did so, then reached up a tanned hand to massage the muscles in the back of his neck. Nerida suddenly saw that there was trust and respect between the two men, and realised that until now she had been too busy with her own antagonistic feelings towards the doctor to perceive the relationship he had with his other colleagues.

'Sam not too heavy for you?' queried Leigh, turning back to Nerida.

'No,' she smiled. 'He's small for his age, isn't he?'

'Yes, he is. It'll be good to have him in Benanda for a bit. We might do some tests. Below average size isn't necessarily a worry if a child is healthy, but with this one . . . there may be a problem we haven't picked yet. He's bright and charming too, when he's well, so it's a pity.'

'It'd be difficult for the O'Loughlins if there was something wrong, wouldn't it?' said Nerida. 'So isolated . . . If he needed regular treatment.'

'Yes.' He shifted his shoulders and faced the front of the plane again.

Not a man who believed in small talk, Nerida was rapidly concluding. Or was it simply the fact that he disliked her? If she hadn't felt the same about him, the answer to this question might have hurt a little.

Coolamon Creek homestead was not as well kept as Patamunda; Nerida could see that straight away as they came in to land. There were outhouses scattered at ill-planned intervals, and several bits of rusty machinery lying about. However, the vegetable garden looked positively luxuriant, which was a nice sign, and flowering creepers covered tank stands and verandah posts.

From this height and angle it looked as if the waters of the swollen creek were at the very doorstep of the homestead, but that had to be an optical illusion.

The airstrip was bumpy, and Jim swore under his breath as he negotiated the landing. Sam woke up at the first jolt and immediately began to cry, called for Mummy. Nerida had already tried to explain about going to stay at Auntie Kath's, and Annie O'Loughlin had too, but it was clear he had not understood, so she didn't try to tell him again but began to talk about other things—a flock of birds they could see from the window, and what sort of things he liked to eat.

'No need for you to come with us,' said Leigh, turning to Nerida again. 'This stop should be a quick one. We're just picking up Margaret Kelly and her two children, and we're only a couple of hundred yards from the house. But you could take Sam for a stroll if you need to stretch your legs.'

'Yes, it might quieten him down,' Nerida nodded.

It seemed that she and Leigh were beginning to establish the tiniest piece of common ground through talking about the child, so she took up his suggestion immediately, and actually followed fairly closely behind the two men as they headed for the homestead building with the capable, energetic strides of people who had been in a bush environment for a long time.

Beneath the white denim jeans he wore, Leigh Russell had iron-hard thighs and calves, and his bearing was upright and even. Jim Stenning, considerably shorter, loped a little crookedly, but he was strongly built too.

No one came out to meet the two men—Nerida had

fallen behind by this time, burdened as she was with the unhappy Sam—and she wondered why. Should she go in? If she did, Mrs Kelly might feel compelled to make her a cup of tea, and Leigh wanted to get away again quickly, so perhaps it was best not to.

Nerida decided to wander for a few minutes among the outbuildings instead. Perhaps she'd find something interesting that would distract Sam from his longing for 'Mummy'.

She had arrived at the scattered collection of buildings now, and felt a chill run down her spine at what she saw. It had been no illusion in the plane that the water was only a few feet from the house. It was fact. The ageing homestead building and its outhouses were nestled in a slight curve of ground that ran parallel to a bend in the creek. By the line of gums Nerida could see that this creek would normally be two hundred yards away, but it had broken its banks and was evidently still rising.

A few inches more of height and the nearest buildings would have their floors threatened, another foot and the floor coverings of the main house would be sodden. And flood levels were expected to peak several feet higher, Leigh had told Nerida earlier this morning in the plane. There was something menacingly impressive in the sight of the slow swirl of water, grey from the clouds it was reflecting, which seemed to have lowered again.

Clearly this evacuation was an urgent one.

Nerida turned towards the house in case, after all, there was something she could do to help. Perhaps Mrs Kelly still needed assistance in moving as many of her possessions above the reach of the waters as possible. She wondered where Mr Kelly was. Doing something to attempt to save the cattle, no doubt.

A cluster of people had emerged from the main building when Nerida reached it. The pregnant woman who was talking to Jim must be Mrs Kelly, and her two children stood defensively near her, holding her skirt. But there were two other people as well: an old man, weatherbeaten and frail and badly dressed, and an aboriginal child who must be about ten, with huge warm black eyes and skinny, knobbly-kneed legs beneath his inadequate cotton shorts.

'You'll have to leave two of those suitcases behind, I'm afraid, Mrs Kelly,' Jim was saying. 'We're over-crowded as it is now, with Sandy and Joe, and we might have a couple more to pick up later on.'

'So I can only take one. All right,' she nodded philo-sophically. 'I'll have to re-pack it, though.'

'Will it take long?' asked Leigh.

'A few minutes, if we're in a hurry,' she replied.

'Good on you!'

'Get the others to the plane and I'll wait with Margaret to carry the suitcase for her,' Jim Stenning suggested.

'Fine,' nodded Leigh.

'What can I do?' Nerida put in. The doctor turned, only then aware that she had approached.

'You?' Unconsciously—or was it?—the monosyllable was dismissive. 'Just go back with us to the plane. You're carrying Sam, that doesn't give you a free hand to do much else.'

'No,' she admitted, feeling a little foolish. She caught a brief, curious glance from Margaret Kelly, then the woman's brow cleared, evidently at the point where she realised who Nerida was—the new nurse from the city, to take Jenny Walters' place.

'Go on then, kids,' ordered Mrs Kelly. 'You too, old Sandy, off to the plane.'

'Eh?' the old man quavered.

'Go and get in the plane,' Mrs Kelly repeated loudly and distinctly.

'In the plane?'

'Yes. Go with Lucy and Ross.'

'Come on, old Sandy,' the eight-year-old flaxen-haired girl said, cheerfully and matter-of-factly, holding out a hand to him.

He took it and shuffled along at her side, clearly not yet comprehending what was going on. Margaret Kelly shook her head.

'He's bad today, very vague. Some days he's quite on the ball.'

Joe hadn't set off with the others. He seemed to be hanging back, and Nerida saw that he was virtually standing on one foot, while the other was wrapped in a dirty makeshift bandage.

'Let's get on with re-packing that suitcase,' said Jim Stenning, and he and Mrs Kelly headed back inside.

Leigh squatted down in front of the small aboriginal child. Nerida knew she should be returning to the plane, but still she hesitated, curious and concerned for Joe. Why was he here? Who did he belong to? Where was his family?

'Sure you won't let me look at that foot now?' She asked.

The boy shook his head shyly but firmly.

'It's hurting, though, isn't it? Mrs Kelly told me you didn't sleep at all last night.'

'Be all right soon,' said Joe.

'Let's see you walk on it, then.'

His expression still guarded and shy, the thin-limbed boy set off gamely, but after only one step on the injured foot, he was favouring it so markedly that he was almost hopping.

'I think perhaps you need to hitch a ride, little mate,' Leigh told him, and in a moment the youngster was riding piggyback, his arms wrapped around the doctor's neck and a wide grin spreading slowly across his features at being carried like this by the flying doctor himself. Nerida set off at his side with her own burden, and risked a bold question.

'You'll have to do something with that foot, won't you?'

'Of course. In the plane, as we fly. No sense in making a big thing of it right here and now.'

'What happened?' she asked.

'He crushed it somehow, didn't you, Joe? Margaret says his mother brought him in last night. She lives on a settlement about ten kilometres away, and is married to one of the stockmen here. When she found out we were due today she wouldn't let Margaret touch it, she insisted on waiting for us.'

'Where's his mother now?' asked Nerida.

'Back at the settlement. She stayed all night, then walked back early this morning.'

'They don't have to evacuate, obviously.'

'I'm not sure what they're doing.' Leigh spoke rather grimly. 'I'm not happy with the way this whole thing is being carried out, as you may have gathered. Reginald Harris has got his own system—supposedly, and no one else is allowed to take any initiative themselves.'

'But surely centralised planning is better than having the right hand not knowing what the left hand is doing,' Nerida returned, mildly but with conviction.

She thought of the many thankless tasks and unpopular roles her father had taken on in his local community since retirement, and how often he had been blamed and criticised for things that were not his fault at all, simply because, as the organiser, he had been the easiest target. Leigh Russell was probably just power-hungry, or perhaps he wanted to be a hero.

'In this case, I don't think the right hand knows what the *right* hand is doing,' Leigh was saying.

'And of course you could do it all so much better.'

There was a beat of blank silence, in which their two sets of footsteps crunching and squelching across the wet bare ground was the only sound. Sam had fallen asleep again, against Nerida's shoulder, and Joe simply looked ahead at the plane with his shy dark gaze.

'Yes, I think we could,' Leigh replied firmly. 'Jim and I, that is. Ask him and you'll find he'll agree.'

Nerida opened her mouth to say that she had no intention of pressing the point in such a way, but at that moment old Sandy and the two children turned around and stopped to wait only a few yards ahead, having reached the plane.

Five minutes later Margaret Kelly was safely seated

up the front next to Jim, with Sam on her lap. Sandy and the children were squeezed as safely as possible in the back, and Leigh and Nerida sat beside the aboriginal boy, in the ambulance-like section behind the seats, ready to examine and treat his injured foot as soon as the plane was safely in the air.

For a few moments Nerida wondered whether they ever would be safely in the air. The extra weight of the new passengers, coupled with the rain-soaked slipperiness of the airstrip, had the plane lumbering and skidding, but finally they were airborne.

'That was exciting!' eight-year-old Lucy exclaimed, and six-year-old Ross echoed the opinion with an energetic nod and laugh. The unconscious trust that lay behind their attitude touched Nerida.

'They have no idea we're in any danger,' she realised. 'And for that matter, I don't know, either, how real the danger is. It might just be my foolishness to be frightened.'

But Jim Stenning's words as soon as they were safely airborne confirmed that the danger was real.

'I think we'll head back to Base, eh, Leigh? If you think of Jerilda . . .' He looked quickly round at Leigh for confirmation of the decision, and the doctor only nodded, a curt clear gesture. 'I'll radio in now and let them know.'

He switched a control and called an identification, then a tight-throated staccato voice came on to the frequency.

'Harris here. That's you, is it, Stenning?'

'Yes, mate, I just gave the Air Doctor Three call sign,' Jim replied.

'Of course.'

Nerida saw that Leigh was listening intently, grim-faced, and heard him mutter under his breath, 'What's that idiot doing at our base?'

'Is Martin . . . ? No, never mind,' said Jim Stenning. 'Just calling to let you know we're coming in sooner than planned. We've got a full load.'

'Where are you coming from, Air Doctor Three? Jerilda, I hope, if you're on schedule.'

'No, we've had some delays,' Jim explained into his microphone, his voice steady above the drone of the aircraft. 'We went to Patamunda first, and we've just stopped at Coolamon Creek.'

'Then I'm afraid I can't allow you to proceed to Base.'

'What?'

'I can't allow you . . .'

'Yes, I heard you, mate!' Jim was impatient now. 'But what do you bloody mean "you can't allow . . ."?'

'I mean that there's a seriously ill patient to be collected from Jerilda at the earliest possible opportunity.'

'There is? Why didn't you radio through that information at a prior time?—God, I'm sounding as pompous as him now,' Jim added parenthetically after releasing the transmitting switch so that the Brigadier could not hear.

Nerida felt a change in the flight of the plane and guessed that Jim had already begun to set a new course for Jerilda, in spite of his apparent belligerence over the way the news was being relayed.

'According to the schedule I prepared for you, you should have been at Jerilda by now,' Brigadier Harris was saying.

'Yes, but in these conditions you can't guarantee that things are going to go to plan, and it was you who cut Tingaringi from . . . Anyway, never mind. Where's Martin?'

'I've deployed Martin's resources elsewhere.' The tone was defensive now.

'Right.'

'Ask him who it is,' Leigh interrupted urgently. 'If it's serious, of course, and if Air Doctor Four is where it should be then we've got no choice, but if we know exactly what's wrong, who's in trouble . . .'

'Who's the patient, please, Brigadier, and what's the story? How serious is it?'

There was a slight pause and a rather nasal breath into

the radio at the other end, then, 'I'm afraid I don't have that information on hand at the present time.'

'He means he doesn't know,' interpolated Jim Stenning, deadpan.

Leigh gave an angry bark of sarcastic laughter, then spoke. 'We can't take any chances. We've got to assume it's really urgent. Tell him we're on our way.'

There was a small silence in the plane. Sam and Ross had dozed off, and old Sandy was still in a vague, dazed state, but Margaret and freckle-faced Lucy were both round-eyed and alert, as was shy Joe, the pain in his foot forgotten for the time being. No one asked any questions, however.

'Let's have a look at that foot, young Joe.' Leigh was the first to speak. His tone was hearty, but it was only a performance. 'Sorry you've had to wait so long.'

''s OK,' the boy said shyly. 'Dun't hurt much now.'

By some miraculous nursing instinct, Nerida found the equipment she needed without difficulty in the cramped but carefully packed stowage holds of the plane. Leigh was carefully removing the now-filthy piece of rag that covered the little brown foot.

Nerida's breath hissed in between her teeth as she saw what was beneath it. Somehow the foot had been badly crushed and was now grotesquely swollen. They didn't know the whole story, but that wasn't important. It was the result that mattered, and the result was a mess.

'We'll clean it first,' Leigh said to Nerida in a low voice, after nodding approvingly at the sterile swabs and basin of antiseptic she had prepared. 'Then I'll give it a proper check, but I'd say there are at least two meta-tarsals broken, perhaps more. Without X-raying it, I can't tell if they need re-setting. It's a damned . . . If only we were heading straight back, and not detouring to Jerilda.'

'There's something wrong, isn't there?' Nerida asked urgently. 'Something you and Jim aren't talking about.'

Their heads were bent close together over the boy. He lay patiently, now that he had accepted the doctor's insistence on looking at the injury, with a sound of pain escaping his lips only every now and then as the antiseptic strung the raw wound, followed by the probe of forceps as Leigh extracted some gritty pieces of sand and dirt, and then fingers as he attempted to find out exactly what damage had been done.

Nerida had not been this close to Leigh before. She was acutely aware of it, aware of the blue of his eyes, of his thick hair, of his tanned and muscular forearms. It was only the discomfort of being with a man she disliked, she told herself, coupled with the fear and apprehension she was continually swallowing back.

He hadn't answered her question, and it was deliberate. His blue stare was cool, and there was a faint smile on his lips that said clearly, 'Are you sure you really want to know?'

'There is, isn't there?' she insisted, and met his gaze unflinchingly. 'Surely you owe it to me to tell me. I'm in this too—on the professional side, I mean. Even if you don't want to tell the others, the patients . . .'

Her initial urgency trailed away into lameness. After all, how professional was she, really, in this situation? Margaret Kelly, and even little Lucy, and Joe in his different way, must know ten times as much as she did about the dangers of the outback in flood time. Nerida could rally round and provide basic nursing care when it was needed, but what other skills or capabilities could she claim to have? Leigh's hesitation was realistic and, in a way, kind.

'It's nothing,' he said finally. 'Simply the nuisance of having to pick up an extra patient when we're already overcrowded, and when I don't know—and can't imagine—who it is or what's wrong.'

'I see,' nodded Nerida slowly.

She didn't believe for a moment that this was the whole truth, and she could see that Leigh knew she didn't, but they both let the matter rest. He even smiled faintly when he realised that she wasn't going to probe any further, and she couldn't help returning the expression with a wry twist to her well-shaped lips. Strange to have an unworded understanding like this with a man she didn't even like!

He was continuing in a lighter tone now. 'As far as I was aware there were only the Winthrop family there, Mr and Mrs and their two teenage girls. They're from Melbourne, haven't owned the place very long and aren't running any stock at the moment. Amber Winthrop—the fifteen-year old—is anorexic, and there was some notion that she wasn't strong enough to evacuate overland. Again, Harris has teed it all up without adequate reference to us . . .'

He sighed between clenched teeth and did not continue. Having heard the pompous ex-Brigadier on the two-way radio now, Nerida had modified her earlier instinctive defence of the man. Her father would not have spoken or behaved in such a way, covering for his own ignorance by an elaborate turn of phrase like a politician. But still, there must be some logic in the way the arrangements had been made, surely!

There was little conversation for the remainder of the flight to Jerilda. After Leigh had finished his meticulous examination of Joe's foot, Nerida dressed it with antiseptic, soothing cream and sterile gauze. It was a difficult task; the flight was a bumpy one.

'Air turbulence,' muttered Jim. 'Sorry, everyone— but at least it looks as if there's clear weather for a spell after this lot.'

But when the dressing was done, Nerida felt satisfied that Leigh would not be able to be critical of it, and any opportunity she had to prove herself not entirely incompetent was welcome to her in these increasingly tension-filled circumstances. Occupied as she was, the flight seemed short, and they were already descending by the time the task was done. Joe smiled an incredibly white-teethed smile, Nerida packed the equipment away, and then both waited for the plane's first contact with the ground.

Leigh was staring intently out of the window, and when she glanced at his hands, which gripped the back of the seat in front of him, Nerida registered with horror that the knuckles were white. She looked at Jim. His concentration was intense, his shoulders hunched forward.

Old Sandy looked drowsy. Lucy and Ross were asleep, curled together in closely-confined discomfort. But all three were well fastened into their seat-belts. Mrs Kelly had bent her heavy body over Sam protectingly, her carry-bag clutched forgotten in one hand. Her eyes were tightly closed and her lips moved.

'She's praying,' Nerida realised.

This was the thing that Leigh and Jim had not spoken of, but which had filled their minds ever since Brigadier Harris's instruction that they were to go to Jerilda. Something about this landing. Was it the plane? Had it been damaged somehow at Coolamon Creek?

'Head down between your knees, Nerida, Joe. Brace yourselves—like this. We haven't got belts, remember,' said Leigh. He helped Joe into a special brace position which Nerida quickly copied, and which he then assumed himself.

Just in time. Leigh had deliberately left his warning till the last minute—to avoid panic, she guessed. There was the usual jolt of landing, only as rough as she would have expected, and she wondered what all the fuss was about for a moment.

Only for a moment. Suddenly the plane began to slew to one side and career crazily. Jim was too involved even to swear, fighting wildly with the controls to try to keep on the runway. A roaring arc of water seemed to be pounding against the windows on one side, then on both. At least this had the effect of slowing them down more quickly.

But by this time Nerida had completely lost track of

what was happening. Instinctively she had closed her eyes and became too disorientated to remain in the braced position she had adopted. There were screams from the children and a groan from Margaret Kelly. Sandy moaned helplessly, jolted out of his vagueness by sheer terror. There was a rending crunch and screech of metal on one side of the plane and a moment later it was all over.

They had come to a halt. One engine gave a slow dying whine, the other had already sputtered violently into silence. Nerida was dazed, and the tangle of limbs that surrounded and entwined with her own didn't quite make sense. Then she realised. Those were Leigh's arms around her shoulders, and her head was pillowed in the sweet yet masculine-scented curve of his neck.

For a fleeting instant she knew an intense desire simply to remain there for ever, not to find out what had happened, what state they were all in, not to have to start coping. His arms were so firm and sheltering, the rise and fall on his breathing so reassuring, but then he stirred and Nerida came to herself.

After that wild careering halt someone could be injured, trapped somehow, in need of help. She opened her eyes. Leigh had already eased himself away, and she saw that Joe was somehow wedged between them too, his small face expressing cautious relief. Nerida sat up, smiled shakily at him and then met Leigh's gaze.

'OK?' he queried.

'I think so.' She couldn't trust her voice to say any more.

'Lucy? Ross?' His first concern was for others, although Nerida could already see blood welling from an aggressive graze on his face, and a red swelling at his temple. She could not help being impressed. It wasn't necessarily how she would have expected the man to react in a true crisis. Was her dislike of him partly the result of misjudgement?

Lucy and Ross were all right, it seemed. They were white-faced and too shaken to speak, but they sat straight in their seats and had no visible injuries. Sam was sobbing so energetically that it seemed likely he was uninjured too.

'I'm OK,' Jim told Leigh.

'I'm not,' Margaret put in, brightly but very seriously.

'What is it?' Leigh questioned urgently.

'My arm, I think,' Margaret spoke steadily, but there was an undercurrent of fear. 'I fell forward on to the control panel. And I had our cashbox in my carry-bag. I wanted to bring all our papers and cheque books in case the house is destroyed. It's metal, and I think maybe . . . I don't know, I think my arm's broken.'

'Perhaps this isn't the moment, Doc,' said Jim. 'But I really want to check the damage and get the plane turned round ready for take-off. We can't afford to spend too long here. I said they'd built this strip too close to the creek.'

'I know,' Leigh agreed. His eyes were narrowed and Nerida could almost see the lightning-quick process of his thoughts. He had taken cotton wool from the plane's medical chest and was dabbing the blood away from his face absently. 'You'd like us all out and clear, wouldn't you?'

'Yes,' nodded Jim.

'We'll take everyone over to the homestead. We've got to find out about this mysterious patient too . . . Nerida, if you could make a rough sling for Mrs Kelly's arm, and bring Sam. Inflatable splints in the locker there. I'll shepherd the others across. It's not far,' said Leigh. 'This is a nightmare—but at least the Winthrops can calm everyone down with a cup of tea.'

The last sentence was added in a low tone that only she could hear, and even in the midst of these urgent circumstances she found a brief moment to feel satisfied that at last he seemed to be treating her as a fellow professional.

Apart from this, she was strangely without emotion. Shock, probably, and sheer ignorance about what kind of a predicament they were actually in. The plane had been damaged, but Jim seemed to think it would still fly. Leigh thought it was 'a nightmare', but he obviously knew what to do about it. Nerida had a sling to prepare. Well, that was easy enough.

She reached for inflatable rubber splint, gauze, safety pins and tape, as Leigh helped Lucy and Ross and Sandy and Joe from the plane. Jim was already on the ground, looking at one of the propellers, apparently. Sam had quietened a little. Margaret made her way with difficulty to the back of the plane, but in her country-bred freckled face there were both grim determination and deliberate cheerfulness.

'It's probably just a bruise or a sprain or something,' she said.

But Nerida could tell just by the feel of the forearm that it was not. Still, it could be set easily enough in Benanda this afternoon, although it would be painful for the rest of the journey back.

Jim was getting back into the pilot seat as Margaret and Nerida, carrying Sam, left the aircraft to walk the two hundred yards to the homestead building. He gave them a faint, automatic smile, but was clearly too pre-occupied to take much notice of their departure. He reached for the microphone control of the two-way radio and Nerida heard him begin to speak in clipped, businesslike tones.

'This is Air Doctor Three calling Benanda Base. Charlie Delta X-Ray, calling Benanda Base. Come in, please . . .'

Then she was out of earshot.

After all that had happened, the terrain and landscape only seemed like part of a dream, and it was a dream that was already becoming familiar. For the time being the cloud had broken and there were bold patches of bright blue sky visible. Sun shone on the wet leaves of the wide line of gums that marked the normal course of the now-vast creek, and in the bright light, the water was a muddy reddish-brown.

It reached on to the airstrip itself—or at least, it had

flooded the drainage channels on either side. The strip could not have been properly levelled, because one side was more submerged than the other, and this was clearly what had caused the wild slewing of the plane and the arc of water that had been thrown up against its windows on one side.

The homestead itself, a neat and practical collection of modern buildings, also looked dangerously close to the waters, but surely no one would have built it there if it was in real danger, as high water-levels in flood seasons were known these days from past records.

It was a puzzle to Nerida. Was this such a record flood? Not for the first time she had a sense of frustration at being such a fish out of water here—if that metaphor was at all appropriate in the circumstances.

It was only as they neared the homestead building that she realised she had not even thought to look for the damage to the plane, or to ask Jim about it. He and Leigh seemed at once both so preoccupied and so in control.

The gracious, low-slung building with its wide verandahs and polished wooden verandah floors looked out over what would usually be a very lovely vista, Nerida guessed. White-trunked gums shading a sandy creek bed, and perhaps a permanent water-hole, and then beyond the far bank a cliff of rugged orange rock that would glow like fire in the desert sunset. Now, however, the waters reached to within a few feet of the verandah's edge.

Margaret lifted her swollen body, made doubly awkward now by the sling, on to the verandah, and Nerida did the same, putting Sam on to his own feet. He had stopped crying—out of sheer bewilderment, she suspected—and could walk by himself for a change. Over two hundred yards of muddy ground he had been an increasingly heavy burden.

The main door was open, but strangely all the windows were covered by colonial-style shutters, which seemed to be fastened. Leigh appeared in the doorway.

'You're here.' There was a new note of anger in his voice, and Nerida instinctively responded to it.

'I'm sorry—we couldn't go any faster. It was a very slippery walk.'

'And I'm afraid I'm feeling pretty shaky,' Margaret apologised, controlling her voice with difficulty. 'I hope the Winthrops can cope with this crowd of refugees—and give us a cup of tea pretty darn soon,' she finished frankly.

'The Winthrops aren't here,' Leigh said woodenly.

'Not here? Then who . . . ?'

'No one's here. The place was locked and deserted. I fished around and of course they'd left the key under a flower-pot. They're not too cityish for that, thank God!'

'But what about the patient we were supposed to collect?' Nerida asked blankly. For a moment Leigh simply looked at her, his mouth twisted. Then he spoke.

'Your guess, Sister Palmer, is as good as mine.'

'That dreadful Harris man,' Margaret nodded. 'Ron says he couldn't run a chook raffle, let alone an emergency service—but we can't grizzle about local politics now.'

'No, we can't,' Leigh agreed grimly. His cheek had stopped bleeding, but his temple was still swollen. He looked up as Jim came towards them at a loping run.

'Mummy?' It was Lucy's voice from inside.

'Just a minute, love.' The response from Margaret was absent. It was clear that Jim had something to say, and she wanted to hear it too.

'Hasn't been a flood like this since 'thirty-five. That's nearly twenty years ago,' old Sandy said knowledgeably, shuffling his thin body out to the verandah and looking about him with faded blue eyes that at the moment looked relatively clear and almost twinkly.

He seemed more alert and happy than Nerida had yet seen him, and she realised—almost with amusement —that this adventure had roused and interested him for a brief moment, reminding him perhaps of a time when he had been a wild young man roping cattle and camping out on the great overland stockroutes.

But Jim had reached them now, panting and dishevelled.

'The radio's jammed on receive mode,' he told them. 'I can flick the mike button on to transmit, but then nothing happens. It just goes on damn well receiving. We'll have to use the homestead radio. Where's the patient? What's going on at this end?'

'No patient. Harris . . . bungled again, apparently. The whole family's already evacuated,' Leigh summarised tersely, already on his way inside.

Jim followed energetically, with Margaret and Nerida after him, like sheep. Sandy stayed where he was, still studying the flood-waters.

'That was a hell of a big one, back in 'thirty-nine,' Nerida heard him say.

'Mummy!' Lucy called again.

'What is it, love?' Margaret turned her attention to the children, who seemed remarkably patient.

'When are we going to have a drink?'

'Where would they keep their radio?' Leigh wondered aloud.

'Station office, I would think,' said Jim. 'Or kitchen.'

'Not here,' said Leigh, striding into the doorway of the large homestead kitchen. Nerida was keeping her eyes peeled as she followed the two men, although she didn't even know quite what the thing would look like.

'We haven't got much time, Leigh. The water's rising on that strip and we've lost an engine,' Jim was saying as they headed down a passageway.

'God, no! How?'

'Propeller housing hit the wind-sock post when we slewed off—buckled and jammed. We've *got* to get the other plane in within the next few hours to get everyone away or it'll be too late. The strip'll be out of action.'

'This is the office . . . It's not here.' Leigh's voice fell flat.

'Where else?'

'Don't know.'

'Bedroom?'

'Not likely.'

'What's this?' Jim rattled the large metal doorhandle of a room that adjoined the office.

'Store-room,' said Leigh. 'I remember noticing it when we had an overnight stop here last year on a clinic flight. Funny place for it, but it's very secure. Metal door . . .'

He broke off, then strode forward and wrenched at the door too. The two men looked at each other in silence for a second and then Jim spoke flatly.

'It's in there, isn't it?'

'Of course. They've locked everything that's portable and valuable in here,' said Leigh. 'They're from Melbourne. They think it's like the city out here and people are going to come—in the middle of a flood —and go looking for their two-way radio to steal. They'd locked the house too, but the key was under a flowerpot.'

'No hope of the key for this being around?'

Leigh shrugged. 'I doubt it. They'd have taken it with them. And if it *was* around it might be anywhere— under a mattress, in the tea-jar. They'd hide it pretty carefully.'

'I'll check the rest of the house just in case we're wrong.'

'There's a window. Too high and too small to get into, but we could look in and at least know for sure if we were wasting our time. Nerida?'

'Oh! Yes? What can I do?' She was startled to be appealed to so suddenly after the rapid fire of words and calculations that seemed to concern only the two men.

'If I supported you on my shoulders, do you think you

could look inside the store-room window and tell us if there's a radio?' asked Leigh.

'Yes, all right. Of course.' She scrambled after him as he strode to a rear door and unbolted it, then made his way around the outside of the house to a tiny window high up in the wall.

There was no verandah along this side of the building, and bright desert sun was strong on the white walls. The weather had cleared very quickly and it was dazzling after the cool, dim interior. Leigh crouched in front of the wall.

'Put your legs over my shoulders and sit down,' he commanded, and Nerida didn't dare to hesitate, although it was an ungainly and awkward movement in her white uniform.

In fact, she had to hitch it up to her stockinged thighs. Fortunately he wouldn't be in a position to notice. He rose slowly, grasping her knees with muscular hands, to steady her.

'OK?' he asked.

'Yes, are you?'

'Fine. What can you see?'

'Nothing yet,' she admitted, peering through the square of glass. 'It's so dark in there and so bright out here, and I'm blocking the light as I look in.'

'Just wait till your eyes adjust,' he said.

'If you can still hold me . . .'

'You're very slim—scarcely a great weight,' he said drily.

'I can see something now,' she said. 'Lots of things. A motor-bike.'

'Good God!' he exclaimed.

'Several cartons, cans of food, bags of flour, I suppose.'

'Bulk food supplies . . . But the radio?'

'Hang on . . . Yes! At least, a sort of metal box with controls like in the plane. Of course it must be the radio. What else would it be?' Nerida finished, disgusted at her own doubt and hesitation.

'Good girl!' Leigh lowered her quickly to the ground with a slight grunt of effort, then stood up, a little flushed.

So was Nerida. Hastily she pulled her skirt down again. What strong shoulders he had!—Although now was scarcely the time to think of it. A button had come unfastened on his khaki shirt too. But he was moving again, back to the door.

'That's that, then,' he said bleakly.

Jim had emerged.

'Any luck?' he asked hopefully.

'Yes,' Leigh nodded. 'Or rather, no. It's in there. Which means . . .'

'We can't get at it?'

'No hope. The door to that store-room is far too strong. At least it'd be flood-proof. I suppose that's another reason why the radio is in there. But that door'd take some battering.'

'Is it that serious?' Nerida blurted. 'I hadn't realised.'

'It's bloody serious,' Jim replied, wheeling round to her. 'But if you let Margaret in on that, let alone Sandy and the kids . . .'

'Of course not, although . . .'

'This is your province, Jim. I'm in your hands. What do we do?' Leigh said. Jim rumpled his reddish hair and let out a heavy breath.

'We start unloading the plane. All the medical equipment. Seats. Damaged propeller, and excess fuel. Then I fly out and get help—the helicopter from the Tanama gasfields. I go to the nearest inhabited spot, if I can get the plane off the ground at all.'

'The helicopter?' Leigh queried.

'Nothing else'll be able to land on that strip pretty soon.'

'And you go alone.'

'Alone,' Jim nodded. 'Any excess weight lessens my chances—not to mention the risk to other lives.'

Nerida's throat tightened and her scalp crawled although they stood outside and it was still warm. Jim

was talking almost casually about risking his life. This
had never been a picnic, and it had ceased to be an
adventure quite a while ago. Even Leigh had admitted it
was a nightmare. Now, it was a disaster.

'Two of us to unload the plane. How long will it take?'
Leigh was asking. Jim shrugged.

'Three,' Nerida put in quickly. 'Three to unload.
You've forgotten me.'

'I didn't forget you. You'll be looking after Margaret
and Sandy and the kids,' said Leigh.

'Margaret can look after the others,' Nerida said. 'She
already is. She's pretty tough and she's not a fool—she
knows things are pretty serious. I'll be more use unloading the plane.'

'She's right, Leigh,' Jim said. 'Margaret's *not* a fool,
and she's lived in this region all her life. I'll tell her
what's what and you two get back to the plane and start
shifting the medical gear.'

They walked in silence back to the plane. The sodden
ground was steaming now in the bright sun. The air smelt
of tar and slightly salty mud, and it was quite hot. Yet
this was winter! Nerida took off her cardigan and
knotted the sleeves around her waist. Scarcely elegant,
but she couldn't think of things like that now. She waved
several flies away from her face and brushed some curls
of fair hair off her forehead.

The plane still stood where it had come to rest, leaning
drunkenly into the boggy water of the ditch at the side of
the strip, and wedged against the bent and twisted metal
post of the wind-sock.

'If you stay in the plane and pass things out,' said
Leigh, breaking the silence. 'We'll shift the baggage and
the loose equipment first, then unbolt the seating and
the fixed equipment. Jim should be ready to help with
that . . .'

They heard the crackle of the radio as they arrived at
the plane. Jim had left it on and there was a voice coming
through. It was Martin Baird.

'Calling Air Doctor Three. Calling Air Doctor Three.

This is Benanda Base. Come in, please, Air Doctor
Three. Your patient is waiting for you at Jeralba Bore.
Please radio your whereabouts. Repeat—please radio
your whereabouts. Your patient is waiting for you at
Jeralba Bore. Calling Air Doctor Three . . .'

'Jeralba Bore!' Nerida said blankly. 'But this isn't . . .
I thought this place was called Jerilda.'

For a moment there was a grim silence, then Leigh
spoke heavily.

'It is. We've come to the wrong place, and that's
why . . .'

'But Brigadier Harris said Jerilda. We all heard him.
And it was written on your list.'

This time there was no reply at all, and Nerida risked a
covert glance at Leigh. She saw that he was fighting to
master an anger that threatened to erupt with wasteful
force and violence. Jim arrived at the plane and heard
the message, which was still crackling intermittently
over the damaged radio. 'Your patient is waiting for
you at Jeralba Bore. Please radio your position
immediately.'

'Harris said Jerilda,' Jim said. 'More than once.'

'He . . .' Leigh could not finish the sentence.

'So they think we're headed two hundred miles north-
east of here. If I don't get off the ground, and we're
stuck, and they send out search planes . . .'

'They'll be looking in the wrong area entirely.'

'It just means I have to get out, that's all,' said Jim.
'Let's get going with the work.'

Nerida had no idea of how long they worked. When
the medical equipment had been piled at random on the
driest part of the strip, near a corrugated iron shed filled
with fuel drums, Jim and Leigh started unbolting the
seats. She would have tackled the task herself, but there
were only two spanners.

'Start taking the gear back to the homestead,' Leigh
suggested.

Nerida made three trips, gritting her teeth against
tiredness and aching shoulders, ignoring the mud that

had somehow caked on her stockings and shoes now, up to her ankles. She barely paused at the homestead each time. Things seemed all right: Margaret had got the Aga stove going and had made tea, Sandy sat on the verandah sipping a huge mugful of it. Lucy and Ross were playing with Joe.

Somewhere Margaret had found a set of wooden building blocks and a Disney jigsaw puzzle. Sam was feverishly asleep on the couch. Margaret herself looked ill at ease, sometimes pacing uncomfortably, sometimes sprawling awkwardly on the couch, but that was hardly surprising in the circumstances.

It wasn't until Nerida's third trip that Margaret approached her and spoke quietly and matter-of-factly.

'I'm having pains.'

'Pains?' queried Nerida.

'Yes—contractions. Labour pains.'

'Oh, heavens! But you're not . . . are you at full term?' Mrs Kelly did not look big enough yet.

'No, I'm not—that's just it. I'm only thirty-three weeks. The baby can't come yet! Not here . . . It wouldn't have a chance!' The desperation broke through Margaret's careful tone, and Lucy looked up, startled, having detected it. 'That's a lovely house you've built, love.' Margaret was instantly the mother again, reassuring, giving away no hint of anxiety to her child.

'Yes, it's got three storeys,' Lucy said proudly, and went back to her play, evidently satisfied that nothing was the matter.

'Are they bad?' Nerida asked in an undertone.

'Just twinges. But I thought I'd better tell you. I can't help feeling worried.'

'Lie down on the couch, on your side if you can. And don't move,' Nerida told her. 'After the shocks we've had today, this is quite understandable. If you drink some more tea and stay calm, just relax and breathe deeply and it'll stop soon.'

'Will it?'

'Yes. It's all quite understandable. This kind of thing happens all the time.' She was stretching the truth, but it was desperately important to sound confident and at ease, or Mrs Kelly herself wouldn't have a hope of relaxing.

'Will Leigh be back soon?' asked Margaret.

'Yes, pretty soon, so if by some chance they haven't stopped, he'll be able to do something.'

'Oh, good.'

'I must get back,' Nerida said cautiously.

'Sorry to trouble you with it,' Margaret apologised.

'No, you were right, but please, just relax now and drink that tea.'

Nerida felt damp all over as she hurried back to the airstrip across the red ground that already seemed horribly familiar. Her legs were weak too—whether from simple exhaustion or from strain, she could not tell. She remembered that she had slept very badly last night, and last night seemed about a hundred years ago.

When she arrived at the Nomad, Jim and Leigh were draining fuel from the tanks into a forty-four-gallon drum, the damaged propeller had been removed, and the interior of the aircraft was stripped bare.

'That should do it,' said Jim. 'I need a bit of a safety margin.'

They capped the drum and manhandled it back to the fuel shed, then Jim got into the pilot seat and started his one remaining engine. Nerida and Leigh watched from the ground as he freed the Nomad from the wind-sock post and taxied around.

'I'm going to take off back down this way. There's a slight slope—very slight, but I need all the help I can get.' His mouth spread into a wide grin below the red moustache. 'See you two back at Benanda— tonight.'

'Yes, see you, Jim,' Leigh said tightly. 'Good luck.'

Nobody mentioned the fact that he might not get through at all.

Nerida and Leigh watched in silence as he taxied away from them. A light wind had sprung up, adding a chill to the air to compete with the bright sun. Nerida put on the navy cardigan again. Suddenly it felt eerily desolate to be standing out here, and she shivered. Jim was gone, and she knew she would miss the bluff cheeriness of his manner, and the aura of technical confidence that hovered about him. She was alone, now, with a man who at best was distant and unknowable, and who at worst returned in double measure the dislike that she herself felt for him.

Jim was at the far end of the strip now, revving the engine to a scream, and then the plane was lumbering along, leaning to one side, its course needing constant correction as it gathered speed.

Unconsciously Nerida held her breath and clenched her fists, wanting to force it to leave the ground by sheer effort of will. It wasn't rising. It wasn't rising. It was, at last, drunkenly, its engine piercingly loud in her ears. It was away.

She heard Leigh let out a lungful of air. He had been willing and praying as hard as she was. Suddenly she remembered Margaret back at the homestead, and blurted abruptly:

'Mrs Kelly's having contractions, Leigh.'

'What!' he exclaimed.

'Contractions!' She was laughing now. 'Do you realise that we're stuck out here, hundreds of miles from hospital and help, no one even knowing we're here, with a pregnant woman with a broken arm who's having contractions at thirty-three weeks, a senile old man, and four children. Doesn't it almost strike you as rather funny?'

She went on laughing as the sound of the Nomad faded in the sky, and then there were tears too, cascading down her sun-pinkened cheeks, and sobs high in her throat that mixed with the laughter and made her shoulders shake.

'Stop, Nerida!' ordered Leigh. 'Just stop!'

But she couldn't, she was helpless, and a moment later he took a long step towards her and hit her full on one cheek, a stinging slap with the flat of his hand.

CHAPTER FOUR

NERIDA was stunned instantly into silence and an awareness of the fact that she had been hysterical. She was
shaking all over now, but fought to control it and
eventually succeeded. She saw that Leigh was watching
her steadily, his face unreadable as usual.

'I'm sorry.' It came out as a hoarse whisper that rasped
her throat.

Wordlessly he reached out two strong arms and
gathered her into them, cradling her head against his
chest. Then he simply rocked her from side to side,
smoothing stray locks of hair out of her eyes and off her
forehead, then caressing her head as he might have
caressed a cat, the kind of gesture that gave comfort both
to giver and to receiver.

Nerida felt strength and calmness returning slowly to
her limbs. She didn't try to think beyond this moment,
but the moment was enough.

It was impossible to say when the nature of their
embrace changed. Was it when he moved his hand from
her hair to her cheek, and began to mould the line of her
jaw with his soft fingers, soothing away the tingling red
mark left by his hand only minutes before? Or was it
when Nerida's own arms wound around his waist and
began to explore the firm muscular shape of his back?
Perhaps it did not matter. Perhaps it was by mutual
need, communicated only by warmth and touch . . .

Leigh's lips sought hers and found them, soft and
gentle at first, then urgent and abandoned. No words
passed between them, but there was a shared understanding that somehow this wasn't real, was part of
another world, or of a dream. His hands left her face
and hair and come down to her waist, moulding her
hips close to his, exploring the shape of her slim

curves, moving higher again to the firm outline of her breasts.

There was a sudden insistent metallic squeaking which startled them both into an instant recoil. Nerida's eyes, which had been closed, perhaps in an attempt to forget that the rest of the world existed at all, snapped open and she saw that Leigh had turned in the direction of the sound, breathing heavily, his eyes narrowed and his lips slightly parted.

It was the wind-sock. Somehow, in spite of its pole having been bent and twisted, the nylon tube itself was still functioning. The breeze must have shifted and filled it with air, and it was flapping, moving the wire that fastened it to the metal pole and making it squeak shrilly.

For better or worse, the moment between them was irrevocably broken. Once again they were two people who had only known each other for twenty-four hours, but who already disliked each other forcefully. And they were standing on a windy, deserted and flooded airstrip in the outback, with four children and two incapacitated adults two hundred yards away who were totally dependent on their care and resourcefulness.

It made their kiss seem monumentally unimportant, and when Nerida looked at Leigh, she knew with utter certainty that he did not intend to let it happen again. He had already turned on his heel and was striding in the direction of Jerilda homestead. She could only follow him in silence.

It wasn't until they had walked for fifty yards that he broke it.

'That's the last time you're going to give way, Nerida. Is that absolutely clear?'

'Yes . . .' she muttered.

'No more tears, no weakness at all. Surely I don't have to tell you . . .'

'No, that's right! You *don't* have to tell me!' she flashed back angrily. 'Do you think I don't understand anything? Do you think I don't know that lives are

already in danger, and that if Jim doesn't get
through . . .'

'Right—good. I'll say nothing more, then. And Jim
will get through.' He took in a deep breath and let it out
slowly.

Nerida saw that he didn't fully believe her, and for a
moment she collected scathing and indignant phrases in
her mind ready to launch a further verbal attack. How
dare he! When he knew nothing about her!

Then she stopped to think. The fact that he knew
nothing about her was exactly what prompted his
doubt.

'And if I were in his position, would I feel differently?'
she asked herself. 'I've been in Australia less than six
months, and I've admitted I didn't want to come to the
outback at all. What have I done so far to prove myself?
Bandaged a foot, put an arm in a sling, carried a few
things—and gone hysterical in the middle of the airstrip.
No wonder he's got doubts!'

Well, he wasn't going to have them for much longer!
The vow came suddenly, with an intensity of purpose
and resolution that she had never felt before, and it gave
her new strength and energy. She wouldn't waste time
on verbal protestations of her ability, she'd prove it
through her actions.

'We'll come back and move the rest of the equipment
later this afternoon, will we?' she asked brightly and
matter-of-factly.

'Yes.' It was a very terse monosyllable, but Nerida
ignored this.

'Perhaps the first thing for me to do is fix up some
lunch. The Winthrops must have left food in their
pantry—it couldn't all be in that locked store-room.
And it must be lunchtime.'

'Way past,' said Leigh. 'But yes, do that. I'll look at
Mrs Kelly.'

'I told her to stay lying on her side,' Nerida explained
quickly.

'Yes, I presumed you'd do that,' he nodded.

So he did credit her with at least some basic nursing instincts! It was already almost impossible to believe that that kiss had ever taken place. Perhaps it was only her hysterical and overwrought imagination? But no, it wasn't, she knew, as a sudden stab of memory pierced her mind, and her lips tingled again with the sensation of his mouth.

Old Sandy was still on the verandah. He had brought out a wicker chair and was gazing out over the landscape, absorbed in it.

'She's still rising,' he said to Nerida and Leigh as they stepped towards the door. For a moment Nerida was confused. Was this some obscure euphemism for Margaret's contractions? Then she realised that he had the bushman's habit of referring to any and every natural or mechanical phenomenon as 'she', and that he must mean the flood-waters.

'She'll be right,' Leigh replied, falling into the same pattern.

Inside, the atmosphere was calmer than Nerida had feared. All four children were playing happily on the floor, and Margaret lay on her side on the couch above them, supervising and responding to their play. Little Sam seemed quite trusting of her now, and Nerida actually heard him laugh briefly.

But Margaret looked up eagerly as soon as she saw Leigh, and a spasm passed across her earthy features. Nerida's heart dropped. The pains must be still coming.

'Leigh . . .' Margaret began, trying to rise.

'You stay lying quietly, Margaret, and tell me what's happening.'

Nerida went into the kitchen. The Aga stove was still burning, but she added a bit more fuel, filled the kettle and put it on again. This at least was something familiar. Only a year ago she had spent a week in the country with her family in a rented house where there was one of these, used for heating and cooking. It was a massive, solid contraption with insulated covers for the hotplates, which could be lifted to spread a comforting warmth through chilly hands held over them.

Her first thought was toasted sandwiches, but this proved impossible, as investigation revealed that there was no bread. She discovered large crispbread biscuits, though, and a block of cheese, and there were gherkins and pickled onions, and even a hunk of strong salami. She cut slices of cheese and laid them on the biscuits, then topped this with slices of pickle and salami and popped them under the griller. It would be nice to have something hot and savoury. They'd all feel the better for it.

As the cheese began to melt, then sizzle, Nerida examined the contents of the kitchen and pantry in more detail. Margaret had opened a container of UHT milk, and it sat beside a canister of tea-leaves and a bowl of sugar. There was instant coffee too, thank heavens, decanted from a big caterer's tin into a rather nice old jar. There was a gas fridge, but it had been turned off by the Winthrops and Nerida didn't know how to get it going again. Still, surely . . . surely! they would only be here for a few more hours, and the milk would not turn sour in that time.

'How's it going?' Leigh appeared in the doorway as Nerida took the first set of hot titbits out of the griller and put in another trayful. 'Looks good.'

'Thanks. Tea?' Nerida queried, holding the tea-pot questioningly over a row of cups. She found she was starting to fall into the laconic speech patterns that Leigh and Jim and Margaret used.

'Love some coffee. What about the children?'

'Lucy likes tea,' said Nerida, continuing to pour the different drinks. 'But there's lemon squash, too. The boys might like that. How's Margaret?'

'The twinges have subsided a lot.'

'Thank goodness!' she exclaimed.

'I'm not taking any chances, though. She's staying on that couch, and when the plane comes she's going out in a stretcher and straight into hospital.'

'*When* the plane comes?' she echoed.

'Yes, Nerida.' There was a warning in the firm tone, but Nerida rebelled against it.

'Is it wise to be so confident? Shouldn't we be making some plans in case we have to stay here overnight?' she returned hotly.

Leigh's eyes narrowed. 'You assume I'm making no plans?'

'Well, you just said . . .'

'There's a way of thinking that you have to adopt in these situations,' he said with heavy patience. 'It's called "double-think". The writer George Orwell invented the term: it means believing two contradictory things at the same time. I *know* Jim is going to get through, but after this lunch you're making, and after we've set poor long-suffering Margaret's arm, you and I are going to make a thorough tour of this homestead to see what's what *in case* we need more food—and beds for the night—and washing facilities. We're not going to say anything about what we're doing, or why, we're not going to make any kind of fuss, we're just going to do it.'

Nerida looked at him for a moment. The intensity of his speech had surprised her, but she was beginning to realise that he was a man who felt things very strongly. So far, the only emotions she had seen in him were negative ones—anger, impatience . . . She suddenly found herself wondering if he felt as strongly when it was a question of love, tenderness, or passion.

She saw that behind those brilliant blue eyes, behind that tanned brow, his mind was already at work on calculations and plans, but that he was ready at any time to adopt a cheerful expression, a grin for the children, an air of calm and confidence for Margaret.

'Right,' said Nerida. 'I think those crispbreads'll be ready by now, and your coffee must be getting cold. I'll serve up, shall I?'

'Yes. Is there a tray? I'll take the tea through.'

'There's one on top of the fridge.'

Once again the tension that seemed to crackle between them at the slightest provocation was dissipated, but for how long?

It was a quiet meal, and more like afternoon tea than lunch, since it was almost four o'clock. Even the children seemed subdued—tired, probably, after the events of the day. They did not try to eat at the dining table, which was piled high with floor rugs and other furnishings which had been moved to prevent damage if the floodwaters flowed through the house, but sat informally in chairs or on the floor around the fireplace.

Leigh had spread out a rug, and Margaret had earlier arranged a few cushions. She herself continued to lie on the couch, which had evidently been too big and awkward for the Winthrops to try to move higher.

After an initial burst of enthusiasm for having 'melty cheese', Lucy and Ross ate calmly. Joe was silent and shy and thoughtful as ever. He leaned against the couch, with his poor swollen foot lifted on to a cushion to ease the throbbing, but his face looked wan.

'Foot's still hurting, isn't it, mate?' asked Leigh, noticing it. The boy nodded. 'We'll do something about that after lunch, won't we, Nurse Nerida?'

'Yes, we will.'

With patient coaxing Nerida got Sam to eat an acceptable amount. His little face was still flushed and scratchy, and he whimpered periodically, but fortunately did not ask about his mother or cry for her.

Old Sandy was the only one who seemed not to like the food she had prepared. His weatherbeaten old nose wrinkled suspiciously. 'What's this stuff?' he demanded.

Margaret explained and he took some cautious bites. His wary expression did not fade, as if he expected some nasty surprise to await him at every mouthful, and Nerida had to suppress a smile. She saw Leigh's thoughtful and narrow-eyed expression soften a little too. Old Sandy had probably lived precariously on damperbread, tinned meat and tea for the past fifty years, with just enough fresh fruit and vegetables to stave off disease and illness. She wondered exactly who he was and where he belonged—if he belonged anywhere.

After everyone had finished eating, Nerida cleared plates and cups into the kitchen, leaving them piled neatly on the sink. The washing up could wait. There were more important things to do.

After giving Joe an analgesic, Leigh had found a low coffee table and positioned it at Margaret's side, removing the sling and inflatable rubber splint that had immobilised her arm until now and had left her relatively free from pain, and laying her arm along it.

Lucy and Ross had been sent out to explore the garden and outbuildings, Joe was lying quietly on a cushion on the verandah with Sandy, who was back in his wicker chair, and little Sam had fallen into a fitful doze again.

'I'm glad things are quiet,' said Margaret. 'Is this going to hurt much?'

'Leigh's going to give you an injection to stop the pain,' Nerida told her. 'We're going to try to align the bones correctly again, which means applying traction—pulling on it—and that would hurt if you didn't have what's called a brachial block.'

She was opening packets of gypsona bandage as she spoke, and had a bowl of water nearby, too.

'That's clever, isn't it?' Margaret said. 'You soak the bandage in water, and the plaster softens, then you just wrap it around. Like papier-mâché.'

'That's right,' Nerida smiled.

'Ready for a bit of a pinch,' asked Leigh, his syringe prepared.

'For a great big sting, you mean?' Margaret laughed comfortably.

She was going to be a godsend if they were stuck there for any length of time, Nerida realised.

'Ouch!'

'All finished,' Leigh said. 'We'll wait a while for it to take effect, but meanwhile, how are those pains?'

'Still a twinge every now and then,' Margaret told

him, soberly now. 'And I'm a bit worried about what'll happen when I need to . . . you know.' She hesitated, embarrassed. Leigh caught her meaning at once and nodded.

'It could be a problem. You must be very careful not to strain, and you'll need to be extra aware of diet for the rest of your pregnancy. Lots of fruit, and plenty of bran and prunes for breakfast.'

Nerida could not fault his bedside manner, although the perverse, rebellious part of her would have liked to. She had to be glad that he was so level-headed in this crisis, and that he seemed to have many talents other than those of a doctor. He had wielded a spanner to unbolt the fixed equipment in the plane with as much skill as Jim, and he seemed to be able to find a level of communication with all sorts of people—bush-talk with old Sandy, a gentle camaraderie with shy Joe . . .

And even with me, she realised, he just keeps safely to medical subjects, unless he *has* to talk about something else.

'Ready, Nerida?'

Taken by surprise, she nodded, and then found she wasn't quite sure what he wanted. Leigh saw it straight away and guided her hands into the correct position on Margaret's arm. His fingers were cool and dry, but to her embarrassment, her own had become slightly damp. It was a relief when his hands moved away.

'You hold steady, and I'll apply the traction,' he said.

'Right.'

'Here goes!' He took a firm but gentle grip and slowly began to pull and twist. 'Just breathe steadily, Margaret, and relax as much as you can. Best to close your eyes too.'

'Is it coming?' asked Nerida. Her muscles were beginning to cramp because of the awkward position she was in and she was starting to be afraid that her grasp would slip at the crucial moment.

'Not yet. Can you hang on?'

'Yes,' she answered him, praying that it would turn out to be the truth. Without having been able to X-ray the break, they were working very much in the dark in any case. Leigh had found out as much as he could about how the broken bone was displaced, but nonetheless there was a greater risk than usual that it would knit together badly—if they could manage to re-align it at all, that was.

'It's coming. Don't slip now, Nerida, for heaven's sake . . . There! That feels like it. You can let go now.' Leigh examined the area of the break, while Nerida dropped her hold in great relief and began shaking out her limbs. 'We'll X-ray it back at Benanda, but I think it'll be fine. It's lucky it was a clean break. Now, Nerida, when you've finished having convulsions, you can start soaking the plaster bandage.'

It wasn't a particularly funny remark, but there was something about the mild tone in which it was uttered that rendered Nerida—who had pins and needles in one arm, a cramp in her calf, and a crick in her neck—even more helpless than before. Leigh grinned too, then laughed openly, and Margaret actually had tears running down her cheeks.

'I'm sorry,' Nerida gasped. 'That coffee table was so low, I couldn't get comfortable. My muscles are all in knots and I'm just trying to shake them out!'

'It's your face, love,' Margaret explained. 'And Leigh's. You both tried to look as if nothing was happening, and as if you were trying to keep your dignity in front of the patient. You were hysterical!'

Nerida caught the flash of Leigh's blue eyes and flinched away from the naked awareness in their exchanged look. She knew that Margaret's last words had made him think, as she was, of that awful scene out on the airstrip less than two hours ago when she really had been hysterical.

'We probably all just needed a good laugh,' Margaret finished.

'I'm sure we did,' Leigh nodded. 'And you managed

to keep your arm still while you were doing it, which is a miracle. Plaster, Nerida?'

'Coming right up!'

It was wonderful what a difference it made to her whole outlook to be working with Leigh when he was in a cheerful mood like this. Not that it meant she had changed her basic opinion of him, she reminded herself hastily. Parts of her still smarted over the rudeness of his initial welcome and his terseness and scepticism at intervals over the long day. Perhaps there were some mitigating circumstances, she admitted now, but not enough! As for that kiss, she did not understand at all how that had happened.

Soon the plaster had been built to sufficient thickness and firmness, and it was simply a matter of waiting until it had dried thoroughly before it was safe to move the arm.

'But since I've got to lie here like a snake on a log in any case, that's no hardship,' said Margaret. Lucy's voice could be heard at that moment: 'I *told* you they weren't big enough to pull up yet, silly!'

'And the kids are obviously all right,' said Leigh. 'Nerida, we'll take that tour of the house now, I think.'

'Right.' She was packing the equipment away as she spoke, and was soon able to follow him out of the room. He stood waiting for her, his face drawn tightly into a frown again, and hard creases at the sides of his mouth. It irritated Nerida, but she would not admit to herself that mingled with this irritation was a prickle of fear. It was when he was frowning that he was liable to be angry with her, treat her as an incompetent fool, and Nerida didn't like that at all.

'So your good humour was just a front for Margaret's benefit?' she said, with a lightness of tone that wasn't sincere.

'No, it wasn't,' he growled, his mouth twisted. 'It was quite genuine. It was fun doing that plaster—like mud pies. I felt as irresponsible as a child for a minute or two. Didn't you?'

'Yes,' she admitted. 'It was nice.'

'But I've just looked at the time.'

'Oh.'

'It's after five. It'll be dark soon.'

'And they won't send out a helicopter after dark to land on that strip.'

'No,' he agreed.

'Does that mean Jim hasn't got through?' asked Nerida worriedly.

'Not necessarily. There could be all sorts of other reasons. And we may well not be their highest priority. After all, there's the patient at Jeralba Bore.'

'Of course—I'd forgotten.' That meant they were definitely spending the night here. Well, it would be comfortable enough, and unless Margaret Kelly's baby renewed its demand to be born, there was not a great deal of danger. Nerida wondered about the mysterious patient at Jeralba Bore, and hoped that he or she was as well off.

'What are you thinking, Nerida?' asked Leigh, studying her narrowly.

'Oh . . . nothing. It's just that the situation seems to change so fast, and I've got so little knowledge to fall back on. It's not that I'm panicking, but . . . the day before yesterday I was in Sydney. I didn't know that any of this existed. It's bewildering!'

She spoke simply, her pretty brows drawn together in a neat frown, not realising that this was the most honest statement of her feelings she had yet made to him. They were standing together in the dim passageway that led to the office, bedrooms and bathrooms. Nerida was unconsciously leaning against one of the doors, her hand absently clutching the round knob, a secure shape, and her cheek pressed lightly against the cool surface of the door's edge.

For a moment, after her words, Leigh's face was soft, as if her confession had touched him, but then he stiffened and turned to walk ahead again.

'You're doing all right,' was the final rough reply,

flung out in haste, as if he resented the wasting of even a
second.

'What have I done now?' Nerida wondered desperately, letting go of the door's support, but she didn't
have time to dwell on it, as their next exchange gave her
a far more tangible cause for concern.

'You'll get a good sleep tonight,' he told her,
'unless . . .'

'Unless Margaret . . .' she began, nodding at his
words, suddenly anxious again to prove that she was
more than just 'all right.'

'No, not Margaret,' he broke in. 'The flood-
peak—the crest. If it comes through tonight.'

'What do you mean if it comes through? The water
isn't rising that fast, is it? We'll be out of here, surely?
before it gets high enough to enter the house.'

He simply shrugged, and turned back briefly to study
her face, the corners of his mouth lifted in what might
have been a smile, except that it didn't go anywhere near
his piercing blue eyes.

'Leigh, you have to tell me!' She was hurrying after
him like a nagging adolescent.

'Margaret and Lucy and Ross can sleep here,' he said,
pausing in the doorway of the main bedroom, his cool
fingers beating out an absent rhythm on the wooden
door frame.

There was a double bed, wardrobe and vanity unit, a
chest of drawers . . . and again the most moveable and
damageable objects had been piled on to the highest
available surface—in this case, the wardrobe. Nerida
could see blankets and linen, a rug, suitcases . . . And
the double mattress had been stood up precariously on
top of the chest of drawers.

'We'll have to fix the beds up later,' said Leigh. He
was ignoring her completely.

'Stop treating me like a child!' It came out shrilly, and
Nerida bit her lip. Was she behaving like one? No! She
did need to know.

'And you can go in here with Sam.' He had stopped at

the second doorway and was surveying the room, which clearly belonged to a teenage girl. Its contents had been dealt with in the same way as those in the main bedroom. Nerida caught up to him, and he added casually, 'You see, it wasn't just the rain in the east. There was a huge storm last week in the catchment area of the river system further upstream. As well as the general rise of the water, there's going to be a sudden crest, a wall of water like a wave moving steadily downstream. Of course the emergency services can estimate approximately when it's going to hit a particular location. Unfortunately, I don't know when they thought it would pass through Jerilda. All I do know is that it'll be some time in the next few days, and will be six or eight feet high. Happy now?'

He grinned cruelly at her and she swept him a scathing glance. It was clear that he was once again expecting hysterical tears. He wasn't going to get them. She set her jaw so firmly that her next words were almost ground out between her small white teeth.

'Perfectly happy,' she said, ignoring the nightmare vision of swirling, foaming waters plunging towards them in the dark, that his words had called into being. 'But wouldn't it be better in that case if we spent the night on the roof?'

They had arrived at the third bedroom. This clearly belonged, also, to a teenage girl, but it was furnished with twin beds and probably doubled as a spare room for guests when the girls were away at boarding school.

'Sandy and Joe should be all right here. And that way, with your room in between the other two, you should be able to hear a call from either side if someone needs you in the night,' said Leigh.

He was ignoring her again, and likewise, Nerida forbore to ask him where *he* would be sleeping, why *he* would be out of earshot, and why, therefore, all the responsibility of night care seemed to be falling on *her* shoulders. She also didn't bother to mention that nothing would induce her to sleep in a bed that might be lifted bodily from the ground by a mass of water while she was lying in it!

Ahead of her, he was opening a door that led on to the side verandah, and from there to some outbuildings, holding it wide for her with exaggerated courtesy. Glaring at him openly, she passed through, and they crossed the yard in silence on their way to the nearest building.

'Not locked,' he said, clearly relieved, as he swung back the wide wooden door. 'We're looking for a ladder.'

'So you did like my idea about the roof,' said Nerida, unable to stop a note of triumph from creeping into her tone.

'Did I ever say I didn't?' Leigh countered lightly.

'You didn't say anything at all,' she retorted.

'Good heavens! That was rude of me,' was his mild reply. It was so exactly what she had been thinking about him that it was difficult not to laugh, but she managed.

He was already searching the barn-like shed. It was filled with farm machinery and some rather surprising odds and ends, much of it new, some of it clearly gleaned from an older dwelling. Perhaps the new homestead had been built on the sight of a pioneer hut of bark or wattle and daub, or rough timber.

The shed smelt not unpleasantly of chaff and leather and coolness, as well as several other smells that had no identifiable source. Light came dimly through the door and through two windows that were partially blocked by objects and equipment leaning against them.

Nerida concentrated on searching for a ladder, feeling a pleased possessiveness about 'her' roof idea, although certain practical problems were beginning to cloud the picture now. Even if they did find a ladder, would Margaret be able to climb it? And Sandy? And Joe? And then what if they spent the whole night up there and no flood-crest came?

But Leigh seemed to be interested in other objects as well.

'Might come in handy,' she heard him drawl, as he set aside several cans of paint and a couple of brushes.

And she was quite startled a few moments later when he suddenly tossed a worn leather stockman's hat and a pair of elastic-sided riding boots towards her.

'Try those on for size,' he instructed.

'Me?'

'Yes, you. They look about right for you.' Again it was a light drawl.

'But why?'

There was a pitying pause and then he spoke softly and lightly, his blue eyes rather heavy-lidded and ironic.

'Poor dear Nerida! Don't you realise that I'm just making this all up as I go along?'

CHAPTER FIVE

'WHAT do you mean?' Nerida queried suspiciously.

'I mean that I've only been in this region for two years myself. I trained and worked in Sydney for years before I came here, although I was brought up in a country town in northern Victoria. But I've never experienced a flood before, let alone in conditions like this. I'm finding your mixture of hostility and touching faith rather amusing—and a little frightening at times.'

'I don't think I want to hear this,' Nerida replied cautiously.

'And I thought you'd appreciate my honesty!' Leigh drawled. He was studying her intently.

'Can't we be serious?'

'I am.'

'Why will I need the hat and the riding boots?' she persisted desperately.

Somehow, the idea that Leigh Russell might not be in control was more terrifying than anything that had yet happened. Surely she could not have been relying on him so strongly, when she disliked him so much?

But she knew that she had been. Beneath the intense annoyance and negative passion she had felt so often in their short acquaintance was a perverse relief at the strength and arrogance of the man. At least they were safe with him! At least he knew what he was doing! And now he seemed to be saying that he did not.

'What's this all about, Leigh?' Her dark eyes had widened behind their long lashes and were almost beseeching.

'Just didn't want you to go on thinking I was perfect, that's all.' A dusty shaft of late afternoon sunlight threaded through his hair and brought the tan to a soft glow on one side of his face, then he turned away.

'You . . . *what*? You . . .' she choked in fury, and couldn't go on.

'Anyway, in answer to your question—since you accused me earlier of *not* answering your questions . . . Have you noticed this boat?'

'That isn't an answer, it's another question,' Nerida muttered.

In the back of her mind was the thought that her anger was caused at least partly by disappointment. For a moment she had actually felt flattered that Leigh was talking seriously to her about something that was important, even if that important something gave her new cause for fear. Now she didn't know what to think. Had he just been teasing? Surely a waste of time and energy in the circumstances! Or had his words been some kind of warning? Or test?

But he was still speaking, having ignored her muttered protest.

'A mile downstream, on the other side of the creek, there's the old homestead,' he was saying. 'It's on higher ground than this.—Here, take these,' he interrupted himself, thrusting the boots into her hesitant hands and dropping the hat unceremoniously on to her bare head. 'There's no ladder in here. We'll try somewhere else.'

He left the shed and Nerida hurried after him, breathless at his sudden changes of mood and subject.

'Why is the *old* homestead on higher ground?' she asked of his retreating back. 'Surely the *new* one should have . . .'

'Yes. Clever girl.' His pace had quickened and he glanced at the wide splash of orange that was spreading over the western horizon. 'The people who built it ten years ago—not the Winthrops, but city people too —liked this site better. The locals told them it wasn't safe, that flood-waters had been known to reach this spot on several occasions, but they said they planned to build a levee—a huge bank of earth—that would protect it. But time went by and it was never done. They went broke, and the Winthrops bought them out, and *they* talked about the levee. They've made plans, but the flood came too soon.'

'So I take it we're going to ferry ourselves across to the old homestead in that boat. Not tonight, I hope!'

'A shrewd guess, Dr Watson.'

'Thank you, Holmes,' Nerida responded thinly.

'And no, not tonight. It'll be quite a task. It's not a very big boat,' Leigh finished drily. 'But the point is, you can't scramble in and out of a dinghy in a nurse's shoes and uniform. You'll be wearing those riding boots, if they fit, and jeans, and if it's a sunny day—which I damn well hope it will be—you'll need a hat. Any more questions?'

'Lots,' said Nerida, glaring at him from beneath the leather brim of her hat. 'I hope you can answer them.'

'So do I.'

They had arrived at the second outbuilding, a shed similar to the first, but smaller. Leigh swung back the door and they were confronted immediately by a sturdy wooden ladder, lying on its side.

'Well, that's one problem solved,' he said easily. 'It looks heavy. Do you mind helping?'

'Of course not.' Her chin came up.

He thrust an arm through the gap between two rungs and shouldered one end, gesturing to her to do the same. They carried it quite easily to the outbuilding nearest the main homestead and he manoeuvred it into position, chocking its feet firmly with some of the stones that bordered a nearby vegetable bed and resting the top against the edge of the flat corrugated iron roof.

'Why not the main building?' asked Nerida.

'Look at the pitch of the roof,' replied Leigh.

'Oh yes,' said Nerida meekly. Why hadn't she noticed herself how steep it was?

'Keeps the house cooler that way. Anyway, this shed'll be protected from the first onslaught of the flood wave by the main building itself.'

'You mean the house might collapse?'

'It's possible,' Leigh nodded. 'To be honest, I don't know how likely it is, but why take chances?'

'So we're not sleeping in those nice comfy-looking beds after all,' Nerida remarked now, trying to make a joke of it, but inwardly appalled at the thought of them all spending the night on that tin roof.

'You are,' corrected Leigh. 'I'm not. I'm sitting on the verandah under a blanket in that wicker chair of Sandy's, and if I hear the flood-crest coming you'll all be woken up and tossed out of those comfy beds and we'll be on to the shed roof like no man's business.'

'Hear it?'

'Yes, it'll make quite a roar. There's a gorge a few miles up, quite narrow. That's one of the reasons why I'm expecting it to come through in such a definite wave. It'll funnel into there and charge through, and the sound of it will bounce off the rock cliffs. With that warning, we should have plenty of time. I'll probably even let myself doze off a bit out there.'

'Then I won't offer to be relief watch,' Nerida said frankly.

'No, don't. You look very tired. Sleep badly last night?'

He reached out a hand and brushed some curls off her forehead, then squeezed her shoulder. Nerida nodded wordlessly, disturbed by the unexpected caresses. She searched for something to say.

'It all sounds very sensible and well thought out,' she finally managed.

'So your faith in me is restored?'

'Almost,' she smiled coolly. 'And it was you who sowed the seeds of doubt in the first place.'

'For a reason, Nerida.' Suddenly Leigh was more serious than she had yet seen him.

'Yes . . . ?' She felt fear leap into her mouth.

'We don't know what's ahead of us,' he said, his blue gaze searching out her own dark eyes with insistent force. 'If something should happen to me . . .'

'What could happen to you?' Her throat was dry and the words were almost a whisper. For some reason the very thought was appalling. Was it simply the aura of danger that his suggestion implied? His shoulders flicked upwards in a dismissive shrug.

'Who knows?' he said. 'But if something did, you'd have to cope alone.'

'There's Margaret . . .'

'Who shouldn't move,' he reminded her with studied patience.

'Or Lucy?'

'She's eight, Nerida.'

'All right.' She spoke almost sullenly. 'But let me face it when I have to. If I have to,' she amended firmly. 'And not before.'

'If that's what you prefer.'

'It is.'

'Anyway, we'd better get going,' he said with a change of tone. 'We've still got the rest of the gear to collect from the airstrip.'

'No hope of the helicopter now?'

'I'm afraid not. The sun's well down. They'll wait till first light now.'

'If Jim has got through at all' was the unspoken amendment in both their minds.

'Aren't you cold?' asked Nerida.

Leigh's comment about the sun had drawn her own attention to the fact that the day's warmth had seeped away. A damp chill struck upwards from the ground on her almost bare legs, and her cardigan was starting to feel too thin.

'Yes, I am actually,' Leigh admitted. 'We'll go inside and check that everything's all right before we go out to the strip. I'll put on something warmer, and you'd better change too. Try out those boots.'

The screen door at the back of the house squeaked as they entered, signalling their arrival to the others, and Lucy called out to them immediately.

'Ross and me've lit a fire. Come and look!'

Everyone was grouped around the cheerful flicker of flames that leapt in the stone fireplace. Margaret lay half-dozing on her couch, a faint smile on her lips and her face relaxed. The warmth and light in the otherwise darkened room was comforting. Sandy had his hands stretched towards the heat.

'She's a good blaze,' he mumbled approvingly.

The children had interrupted their play to observe Nerida's and Leigh's reaction to their work.

'It's lovely,' said Nerida, going to it to warm her hands too, and taking off the hat that she had almost forgotten about.

'We found more wood out the back,' Ross said proudly.

'And Mum told us how to set it properly,' Lucy added.

'How's it going, Margaret?' asked Leigh, crouching beside her couch for a moment, his voice lowered.

'Fine,' Margaret nodded sleepily. 'No pains for over an hour.'

'Excellent!' Leigh said. 'But don't let that tempt you to get up.'

'I won't,' she replied. 'But what's going to happen about dinner and the beds? No one'll come for us tonight, now, will they?'

'No,' said Leigh soberly and matter-of-factly. 'But we've got everything organised for the night, and you're doing a great job here with the kids.'

'Why does Mum have to stay lying down all the time?' little Ross put in suddenly.

'She told us, silly,' Lucy said admonishingly, giving him a stern, freckle-faced frown. 'It's because Baby Karen wants to come and she's not big enough to yet, so she has to stay in.'

'She wants a little sister,' explained Margaret with a smile. 'To be named after her teacher on School of the Air.'

'We had Princess Diana on School of the Air once,' Lucy said to Nerida, making a sudden connection of thought. 'When I was much littler. We lived in Alice

Springs region then. She was visiting Australia. She's from England like you, isn't she?'

'That's right,' Nerida smiled.

'You haven't got any light in here,' Leigh put in. 'I suppose the generator's not running. I'd better see what I can do. Perhaps you could be changing, Nerida?'

'Yes, of course.' She accepted the reprimand in his tone. 'Lucy love, I'd like to hear all about School of the Air, but we'll have to wait because I've still got lots of things to do.'

'Right,' she shrugged cheerfully.

'Why don't you sing some songs for Sam?' Margaret suggested to lively Lucy as Nerida and Leigh left the room.

The things that had already been brought from the plane had been piled haphazardly in the homestead office, and amongst them Nerida found the plastic bag of clothes that Leigh had thrown together that morning. She took them into the room that Leigh had earmarked for herself and Sam, and changed quickly in the gathering dimness. The salmon-pink pullover felt warm and comfortable, and the socks infinitely better than her cinnamon tights which were still flaked with dried mud. The riding boots did fit, and were much more sturdy and practical than her white nursing shoes.

Just as she was ready, she heard a rhythmic thumping start up outside, and guessed that Leigh had succeeded in starting the Diesel generator that powered the electric lights in the homestead. She found the light switch in her room and flicked it. Yes. Good. That would make things easier.

The chorus of pleased voices that came faintly from the lounge told her that they had switched the lights on in there too. She met Leigh outside, coming from the small generator shed at the back. Now, on top of the khaki shirt that had been warm enough all day, he wore a bulky black pullover that contrasted sharply with his white denim jeans and blurred the firm outline of his muscular shoulders and chest. He eyed her own change of dress approvingly.

'Bet that feels more comfortable.'

'It does,' she admitted. 'Does it mean I'm officially off duty?'

He gave a low chuckle and they continued in silence.

It took two trips each to transport the remainder of the equipment, and although Nerida was very tired, she found the journeys strangely pleasant. They hardly spoke at all, but the night was so beautiful that it didn't matter—refreshingly crisp without seeming too cold, now that she was protected by the pullover, and very calm since the afternoon's wind had dropped at sunset.

The sky was a cavern of midnight blue, thick with cold and distant stars. Nerida thought she had never seen them so bright and clear. Then a yellow glow appeared on the eastern horizon and the moon rose huge and golden, dimming the stars but bringing out almost luminous blue tones and highlights on the earth.

She felt strangely at ease with Leigh too, and even the flood-waters, still swelling imperceptibly, almost ceased to hold menace. Until Nerida risked a glance sideways at Leigh on their final trip back to the homestead and saw the preoccupation in his face.

'He's listening,' she realised. 'Listening for the sound of the flood-crest in the gorge.' Involuntarily, she shivered.

'Cold?' He had noticed it.

'A little,' she lied.

'Soon be back inside.'

'What happens then?' she asked.

'I'm giving all the answers again, am I?' he queried calmly.

'No,' she replied meekly. 'I suppose I can work it out for myself. Dinner, and the beds.'

'Yes, and I'd like to sort out the medical gear, get it up as high as possible, then work out what we'll need to ferry over to the old homestead tomorrow.'

'*If* we're still here by then,' she reminded him smoothly.

'Quite.'

'That sounded very English,' Nerida observed.

'Oh, I can mimic you lot passably well,' he drawled. 'Are you at home in that kitchen?'

'Reasonably.'

'Then I'll leave dinner to you and get to work on the rest myself.'

They parted company after depositing their loads in the office. Nerida popped briefly into the lounge to see if everything was all right, and found that it was. The children had found a Ludo board, and Lucy was at present coaxing Sam through his turn with the dice. Margaret had a book, and Sandy was dozing.

'I'm about to start dinner,' Nerida announced.

'Goody gumdrops! What are we having?' As usual it was Lucy who led the chorus of hungry voices.

'Don't know yet,' Nerida admitted cheerfully. 'But I'll find something nice.'

'Sausages,' suggested Lucy hopefully.

'Or soup,' put in Ross.

Soup seemed like a good idea, a nice thick and hearty one. Unfortunately there only seemed to be packets of dried soup-mix, but then she found tins of tomatoes, kidney beans and sweet corn, and added those, as well as a generous cupful of macaroni. She found flour too, and mixed up a batch of scones. The result, half an hour later, was a soup so thick it was almost a stew, and a heartening plate of steaming and gratifyingly light scones.

Nerida went to call Leigh and found him flicking the last blanket expertly over the small camp-bed he had found for Sam. He laughed and turned towards her when she appeared in the doorway.

'I should have been a ward-maid, not a doctor.'

'Hospital corners, I hope,' Nerida said sternly.

'Examine them yourself, Sister, and I think you'll find no cause for complaint.'

'I came to say that dinner was served,' she told him.

'Already? That's great!' The honest masculine appreciation tickled her humour once again and she smiled under the cover of the dark corridor.

'Something's happened,' she realised. 'I don't hate him any more.'

She wasn't quite sure what she felt instead, and for some reason did not want to look at the various possibilities too closely. Suddenly, starkly, she remembered their kiss again. It already seemed like a long time ago, and very unreal. And very foolish and unimportant as well, she added firmly.

The simple meal was soon despatched, and with evident relish on all sides, much to Nerida's relief. Sam did well, and even Sandy spooned steadily away at the soup, and took rather more than his fair share of scones. Everyone except Margaret ate at the kitchen table, as that seemed easiest, and because of the Aga the room was quite warm and cosy.

'How about you and me tackling the dishes?' Leigh said to Lucy when they had all finished, and the sheer novelty of washing the dishes with the flying doctor made her forget to complain about the chore. He turned to Nerida. 'Margaret should get to bed. This afternoon can't have been as relaxing as it should have been for her.'

Nerida nodded. 'And she'll need a bit of help with washing and things. I'll go and suggest it straight away.'

It was well over an hour before everyone was settled. Margaret had needed no persuading, Joe had been shyly obedient, and even Lucy and Ross seemed quite ready to snuggle under the blankets of the wide double bed with their mother.

Sandy had an old man's reduced need for sleep, and seemed very happy to sit staring into the coals of the lounge-room fire, with yet another mug of the strong milky tea that was his preference. Sam was the only one who was difficult to settle. Leigh looked in as Nerida prepared him for bed.

'Poor little mite,' he said. 'He should have been immunised against measles, but the O'Loughlins were away down South when he was due, I remember, about six months ago, and somehow it was overlooked. We would have done it on one of our clinic flights over the next few months, and the Gangali kids too, but it's too late now. It's a pity. Most people are aware of the dangers of diseases like polio, but a lot of people don't know that measles can be a killer too.'

'Yes,' nodded Nerida. 'It's the same in England too. It needs to be talked about more.'

They were both thinking about the degenerative disease that went by the long-winded name of Sub-acute Sclerosing Pan-encephalitis, or SSPE for short. It was a rare and fatal complication of the measles virus that might only occur years after the original disease.

'Two hundred children have died of it in Australia over the past ten years,' Leigh told her.

'That many?' Nerida was surprised.

'Yes, it's twenty times more common here than in Britain, apparently—we don't know exactly why. There's a government campaign running at the moment to make parents aware of the need for immunisation. Still, in this case,' he finished, 'the possibility of SSPE is scarcely our first cause for concern. Have you found something that will serve as a nappy?'

'Yes,' Nerida replied. 'I cut up one of the towels from the linen cupboard. I felt dreadful attacking someone else's property like that, but I looked everywhere and there was really nothing else that would do. The towels amongst our equipment were too small, or not absorbent enough. It's fortunate that he's toilet-trained during the day.'

'I doubt that the Winthrops will begrudge one towel under the circumstances,' smiled Leigh. 'And it can easily be replaced.'

Sam was whimpering behind this whole exchange,

wriggling and protesting as Nerida folded and pinned the
makeshift nappy as best she could.

'You may be in for a disturbed night,' Leigh warned.

Nerida smiled ruefully. 'If it's just this little lamb that
disturbs it, I'll thank my lucky stars.'

Leigh passed on to Joe's room, having said that he
wanted to check the aboriginal child's still pitifully
swollen foot and re-do the dressing. With that kind of
injury, it was purely a matter of time and constant gentle
care—keeping the foot raised so its throbbing and
swelling were less painful, and making sure that in-
fection did not set in, by renewing the sterile dressing
frequently.

Sam's condition was similar in the kind of attention it
needed. Nerida checked his temperature and found it to
be only a little higher than normal, then she applied the
special ointment that was used to treat his eczema. He
seemed to find this last familiar procedure reassuring,
although he did ask about Mummy, as if he had suddenly
been reminded of her.

'We're going to see Mummy soon,' Nerida replied,
hoping desperately that he'd be satisfied with this. 'And
tomorrow you're going to stay with Auntie Kath.
Tonight you're going to sleep in this funny bed, and I'm
going to be just there next to you in the big bed.'

He looked at her, wide-eyed, digesting all this. She
had said it several times during the course of the day,
as had Margaret, and at last it seemed to have sunk
in.

'Mummy likes you,' he said. It was tentative, part
question, part statement.

'Yes, she does, and I like her,' Nerida said lightly. No
point in saying that she had only met Mrs O'Loughlin
once.

'What's your name?'

'Nerida,' she said clearly, also not for the first time.

'Neddie,' he repeated.

'That's right.' It was quite an endearing shortening for
a child to use, really.

'Sing a song?' queried Sam.

'All right, I'll sing a song. You snuggle into bed first and close your eyes.'

She helped him to do this, turned out the main light to leave only a little bedside lamp by her own bed, then sang three gentle little songs she remembered from her own childhood, in a sweet-toned though not strong voice. By the end of the third one Sam was asleep.

A movement in the doorway caught her attention and she saw that Leigh was standing there watching her. When her eyes met his, he mimed some handclaps.

'I liked the one about the donkey,' he said quietly.

'Oh, then you've been there for ages!' Nerida blurted in a whisper, embarrassed for some reason.

''Fraid so. Should I have coughed?'

'Of course not!' She managed a soft laugh, rising to her feet and leaving the low bed she had been sitting on. 'He's got a dear little face when he's asleep, hasn't he?'

'Very. Feeling clucky?'

'No, I just . . .' But she couldn't think of an end to the sentence. Perhaps she had been 'feeling clucky' and that was why she had felt quite exposed when she found he'd been watching her.

'Come out on to the verandah, and we'll have a port,' he invited.

'A port? Isn't that making a little too free with the Winthrops' things?'

'When it's strictly for medical purposes?' he countered lightly, then added in a more serious tone, 'Don't worry, Nerida. The bottle is already opened, and I'm making an exact inventory of every single item we use, consume or damage. Out here, those values about privacy and property blur when there's a crisis on.'

'You've convinced me,' she said. 'A port would be lovely.'

'Bring a blanket to wrap yourself in. It's chilly out

there,' he said, tossing one towards her from where it lay folded at the end of the bed. 'But the moon over the water and the cliffs is so lovely I thought you'd like to see it.'

'I would, very much,' she said.

Somehow the near-exhaustion she had felt earlier had dissipated, and she felt surprisingly fresh and alive. Leigh left her and went off to prepare the port, and, without fully understanding herself, Nerida took a brush out of her sponge-bag and raked it energetically through the fair waves of hair that bobbed about her face, giving them added bounce and a lustrous sheen. She examined her face in the mirror and hovered over the make-up in her sponge-bag before rejecting it in sudden irritation.

How ridiculous to put on make-up for drinking one small port before bed on a flood-bound verandah with a man whom she had loathed utterly only this morning! He would think she was trying to stage some kind of cheap seduction scene. The very thought made her flush with shame and she put her sponge-bag away hurriedly.

She couldn't have started to find him attractive, could she? No, of course not. It was just that, after the trauma of the day, it was nice to be able to relax in a civilised manner, and she wanted all the trappings that went with it, such as being able to feel that she looked her best. Perfectly reasonable of her—but whether it was reasonable or not, she wasn't going to get out that make-up!

They spent much longer on the verandah than she had planned to—over an hour, in fact. It was quite odd how quickly the time passed and how contented she felt out there, because really she wasn't warm, even beneath the blanket. Outback winter days could be hot, but at night, especially a clear night like this, the temperature plummeted.

There was a lot to talk about and catch up on, of course. Background details about the events of the day, a little sharing of information about their own lives, and finally Nerida listened enthralled as Leigh told her what he knew of old Sandy's life-story, in between sips of port.

He was over eighty, it seemed, and had been living a simple life in an outhouse on the Kellys' property for several years, semi cared for by Margaret, but still fiercely independent in some ways, after his fiercely independent life. He had started working as a drover at the age of twelve, back in the days when there was no such thing as the Royal Flying Doctor Service, nor even the Australian Inland Mission's bush nursing homes in this region. Lonely deaths from dehydration, hunger or disease were an ever-present reality, and travel through the region was slow and laborious.

Sandy had been engaged sixty years ago to a young Irish kitchenmaid named Bridget, who worked at an isolated hotel along one of the famous old stock routes in Southern Queensland, but before they could be married she had died tragically. There was no one left now who could tell the exact story, apparently, except Sandy himself, and no one had heard him speak her name for years. He had never married.

'Margaret says he's remained faithful to her memory all these years,' Leigh finished, smiling as if he thought this idea an over-romantic and unlikely one.

'Maybe he has,' Nerida countered, reacting to his tone. 'There are people who are capable of that kind of love—although it seems to be a dying art these days. But perhaps you don't believe that.'

It was dangerous territory, here on this moonlit verandah, with just the two of them and the seductive warmth of the small port she had drunk running through her veins. Leigh's views on love and romance were no concern of hers.

'Oh, I believe that kind of love is possible,' Leigh said slowly. 'But I don't believe it happens very often, and most people seem content to settle for something very much less.'

'It's what you make of it, though, isn't it?' Nerida

countered swiftly. 'Great love isn't just handed to you on a plate. You have to work on it.'

'But you have to have the right material to work on.'

'Yes, that's true.'

Her animation subsided as she suddenly thought of Damon. He seemed a cardboard cut-out figure to her now, not real at all. If they had both worked harder, could they have made a great love out of that relationship? She did not think so, but sat quietly for a few more minutes trying to imagine it, and trying to imagine how the right relationship *would* feel—but as to this last, she found that she just did not know.

'You'd better get to bed, Nerida.' Leigh interrupted her reverie with the words, and she looked up startled, and saw with a pang of surprise that he was scowling out into the night, not turning half towards her as he had been while they talked.

'Had I? Yes, I suppose I had,' she blurted awkwardly, unable to adjust to his sudden change in mood.

'Well, it's nearly eleven, and you were up early.' His blue eyes were narrowed and he did not look at her.

'Of course.'

'Not to mention what we might have to do tomorrow.'

'Yes, I wasn't thinking. Sorry.'

The harmony between them was completely gone, and she stumbled to her feet, letting the blanket slide to the ground in a heap.

'Can you give me that blanket?' he asked, not taking his hand out from under the one that already covered him. 'Just drape it over.'

'All right.' She gathered it up clumsily and spread it over him, wincing inwardly at his expression of irritation because she hadn't laid it down quite right. 'You're going to be very uncomfortable out here all night, Leigh.'

It was an impulsive statement of genuine concern, but it did not re-establish any warmth. He merely settled a little lower in his chair, wrapped the blankets more closely around him, adjusted a cushion and answered tersely, 'I'll be fine. Good night.' It was blunt-toned and not warm.

'Good night, Leigh,' said Nerida, and turned on her heel to re-enter the house.

CHAPTER SIX

IT WAS Sam who woke Nerida the next morning at just before seven. He had woken her in the night too, crying feverishly and needing his nappy changing. After taking his temperature and finding that it had mounted, she had given him half an aspirin crushed in a teaspoon of honey, with a glass of water to wash it down, and he had quickly gone off to sleep again.

On her way back to the kitchen with the spoon and glass, she had glanced at Leigh through the window. He seemed to be dozing lightly, though he very definitely did not look comfortable. She turned fairly quickly away, not wanting him to shift position, wake up and catch her watching him. In the kitchen she stood quite still for a moment, listening for the sound that Leigh was waiting for through his cold vigil, but she could hear nothing as yet.

In the lounge, Sandy had fallen asleep in his chair by the fire. No sense in disturbing him to send him off to his proper bed. He could well be restless and wakeful in the early hours of the morning, and that would only keep Joe awake too.

But she did tiptoe softly into Joe's room and get a blanket from Sandy's bed. The fire had died down now and he would soon start to feel cold, although the Aga in the kitchen still spread quite a bit of warmth through the house. Nerida was just about to close Joe's door again gently when she saw that he was awake and watching her, his eyes very bright in the dark little face.

'All right, Joe?'

'Foot hurtin' a bit. Can't sleep.'

So she gave him another pain-killer, then listened for a minute outside the main bedroom door, but Margaret and the children seemed quite quiet. It was lovely to creep between her own sheets again, satisfied that everything was all right, and it was even lovelier to wake up—admittedly a little too early for her taste!—and realise that the night had passed safely without the unknown quantity of the flood-crest she had secretly dreaded.

When Nerida went out on to the verandah with Sam tucked in the crook of her arm and perched on her hip, after washing and dressing him as well as herself, she found Leigh beginning to unfold stiff limbs from his chair. The sun had begun to creep across the polished wooden floor of the verandah and it looked like the start of a beautiful day.

'Well, we survived the night without interruption,' grinned Leigh, stretching his sculpted muscles appreciatively. 'God, that feels good!'

His strange ill-humour of last night seemed to have faded without trace, but Nerida still felt wary of him. Those last few minutes before she went to bed had made her retreat back into her earlier feelings about him, and she wasn't prepared to let go of the safe mantle of dislike just yet.

'I've put the kettle on and stoked up the Aga,' she said a little coolly. 'I thought I could leave Sam with you while I go and help Margaret to dress.'

'Yes, good idea.' He was distant and matter-of-fact now too. There was a silence while he glanced at his watch and at the position of the sun, and Nerida saw that there was an unreadable shift in his expression. 'I'll take a look at Joe, and I want to give old Sandy a check-up too. He was up three times in the early hours. It's that restlessness that's symptomatic of Altzheimer's disease. I just want to assess a bit more accurately what risk we'll be running with him in the boat this morning.'

'You talk about the boat trip as if it was definitely happening,' Nerida said, trying to speak lightly but not fully succeeding.

'It is, Nerida.' His voice was steady and serious. 'I think we have to accept that now. If our situation had been known last night, a helicopter would have set off well before first light this morning, and it would have been here by now. We wouldn't be *that* low on their priorities! It has to mean that Jim didn't get through.'

Nerida's throat tightened uncontrollably and tears pricked behind her eyes. She clenched her fists and let her nails bite deeply into her palms in the hope that the pain would be a distraction, but it was not. However, she managed to word her question huskily.

'Does that mean he hasn't survived?'

'Not necessarily.' Leigh was staring at the red cliffs beyond the swollen creek, and Nerida knew that he was fighting the same emotion as she was—only of course it would be stronger for him, as he and Jim, doctor and pilot, had been real friends. 'He could have crash-landed somewhere safe, but without access to a radio. We can't know, and we can't expend our own energy in wondering and worrying about it. We've got to think of other people's lives now.'

She could see that he was speaking as much to build and affirm his own courage as to bolster hers.

Breakfast was not a happy or relaxed meal. Everyone except Sam and Sandy understood what was to take place, and even Lucy could not regard it as simply an exciting adventure. Margaret was pale, although she insisted that she had slept well and was having no more pains. Nerida could not help thinking of cheerful, russet-moustached Jim and picturing him in half a dozen nightmare circumstances, although she knew it was foolish and hurtful and useless to do so.

'After breakfast, when there's more to do and less time to think, I'll be all right again,' she told herself, but beneath this was the awareness that she lacked Leigh's support this morning.

He was lost in thought throughout the meal, accepting the steaming coffee she handed him without a word and moulding his strong yet well-shaped hands around the mug with unconscious intensity, as if he needed its warmth and comfort. She knew he was thrashing out the day's plans in his mind, making a dozen important decisions, probably, behind that tanned mask of a face with its rigid frown of concentration.

But whereas she felt that yesterday evening he might have shared some of his doubts and questions with her, or asked her about her own ideas, today he did not. His mind was locked, and his awareness impossibly distant.

'Have another mouthful for Neddie,' Nerida said to Sam, switching off this compartment of her thoughts. 'Neddie' was the name Sam seemed to have settled on for her. She liked it, and its sound coming a little awkwardly from his small mouth made her feel strangely tender.

He swallowed the mush of cereal obediently, leaving his bowl empty, and took a final mouthful of the orange juice concentrate she had mixed up this morning. It was good that he was beginning to trust and respond to her—even if Leigh's feelings seemed to be taking the opposite path!

'I would have liked to go over to the old homestead by myself first before we took any of the equipment, to check that we'll definitely be better off there than here,' Leigh said after breakfast.

He and Nerida were in the homestead office, surrounded by the piles of equipment, food and clothing that needed to be ferried across to the old homestead.

'But we simply can't afford that extra journey,' he continued. 'We've got to keep our trips to the absolute minimum. It'd be different if we had an outboard for the boat instead of oars . . .'

Nerida nodded silently. They had not been able to find any kind of motor for the wooden dinghy, and he had already explained how they would make each trip, using the current to propel them downstream to the old homestead, while gradually steering from one side of the wide body of water to the other.

That was the easy part. It was the return journey that would be difficult. Leigh would be rowing against the current, and it would quickly exhaust his strength.

So it had been decided that he and Nerida would go together with a full load of gear, and he would leave her behind to set up a bed for Margaret, and clean and tidy if necessary, while he returned to bring Margaret and the children, then Sandy and Joe. Finally he would make another journey, or two if he could and if it was needed, to bring over the rest of the things.

The swollen waters had risen still further during the night, at a steady and insidious rate that was only apparent over several hours' interval. It meant, though, that the boat only had to be carried a few metres from the shed before it could be floated around to the front of the house and moored to a verandah post while being loaded.

For this first trip Leigh had chosen an assortment of staple foodstuffs, bedding and basic medical equipment, as well as some special things that, if the worst came to the worst, they would need to deliver Margaret's baby. He and Nerida worked together to pack it as neatly and stably as they could into the bottom of the boat, finding plastic sheeting in one of the sheds with which to protect anything that might be damaged by water.

By common unworded consent, they barely spoke as they did this, limiting their words to the strictly necessary exchanges of instructions and questions: 'This?' 'Over here.' 'It's too big.' 'Move the food box to the stern.' 'That's all right. It feels quite solid.'

Lucy and Ross had routed out some more toys from a cupboard, and yesterday afternoon's scene in the lounge-room was repeated this morning, with Margaret lying on the couch, supervising the children's play.

Only Sandy was behaving differently. He was very vague and restless today, and Lucy had to be sent outside several times to prevent him from wandering off beyond the outbuildings into the barren yet waterlogged desert. She did this each time with her mother's direct and matter-of-fact cheerfulness, but it provided an added note of tension nonetheless.

'I'm going to give him a tranquilliser before I row him

across,' Leigh had said earlier, after he had examined the old man and talked to him for some minutes. 'He wasn't terribly communicative on the subject, but I gather that like a lot of the older people who've lived all their lives out here, he can't swim, and I can't risk him refusing to go into the boat or panicking halfway across and capsizing us.'

'No, indeed!' Nerida exclaimed. It was an awful thought.

Finally, they were ready. Lucy and Ross came out to wave goodbye, and Margaret gave Nerida a rough warm squeeze from her position on the couch.

'Leigh knows what he's doing, love,' she said. 'Just follow his lead.'

'Well, I'm doing that already,' Nerida thought. 'He's cold and distant this morning, and I'm the same—and it doesn't matter a bit!'

She shook off the thought; it was too personal. There was no time for liking or disliking right now. The boat journey was the only thing that mattered.

Nerida sat in the stern looking ahead, while Leigh took his position in the bows with the oars. The sun was already quite warm, and Nerida found that she could take off her fluffy pullover to leave only the pale grey cotton blouse she wore beneath. The leather stockman's hat with its wide brim was welcome protection against glare too.

Leigh wore the blue jeans from his overnight bag and a faded denim shirt, with leather boots and hat that were similar to her own. He was clearly a casual dresser, but the look suited him. The washed-out blue of the shirt brought out his tan, and the hat with its brim tilted down over his sapphire blue eyes made him look like a true bushman rather than a medical man.

He untethered the dinghy from its post and pushed it away from the verandah with an oar. They scraped the bottom slightly at first as the water was very shallow here, but gradually began to move faster, as they started to reach the first pull of the current. Leigh twisted

around on the wooden bench seat and used one oar to
steer them steadily further out.

'No sense in fighting the current,' he said. 'We need to
go downstream, so I'll let it take us there, while we work
our way across. Let's just hope I judge it right.'

'You will,' said Nerida steadily. 'It seems much slower
than at Patamunda yesterday, anyway.'

'Deceptive,' he responded tersely. 'It's smoother, less
turbulent here, but just as strong.'

'I didn't realise.'

He just shrugged in reply and continued to work with
the oar. They were approaching the trees that marked
the usual bank and bed of the creek, so there was more
to do now, making sure the boat didn't slam into one of
the huge white trunks. Nerida saw the rippling play of
the muscles beneath his shirt and heard his breathing
coming faster and deeper.

'Watch out! There's a branch, full of flood debris, a
few yards further down. Just below the surface,' she said
a few minutes later.

'Thanks.' Leigh could only just spare his breath for
the reply as he expertly fended them off the obstacle.

They disturbed several flocks of birds as they passed
—screeching corellas and sulphur-crested cockatoos,
and then a wheeling group of Major Mitchell cockatoos
with delicate coral pink shading beneath their wings that
was visible and then disappeared as they changed the
direction of their flight in unison.

The detail of the cliffs on the opposite bank grew
clearer as the boat approached the other side, but before
Nerida could study the vegetation that clung to the
rust-coloured rock, they had passed further downstream
to where the cliffs petered out into a hillside covered
with wild hops, saltbush and Sturt's Desert Peas that
were not yet in flower.

'Nearly there,' Leigh said, breaking a silence that had
lasted for some time. 'We'll have done it in half an hour.
That's good.'

Several minutes later he had found a mooring against

a straggling tree. The ground sloped quite steeply at this point, and it was a climb of about fifty metres to the old building they were aiming for. Nerida could see why the new homestead was sited on the other side of the creek and further upstream. The outlook from this spot was barren and cheerless, and no trees grew nearby. But it was well out of reach of the flood-crest, and that was what counted now.

'We'll have a look before we get out the gear,' said Leigh, and Nerida scrambled from the boat.

Belatedly, he held out a hand for her, but she was already on the ground, and she saw that in any case his gesture had been automatic courtesy. In every other way he was scarcely aware of her presence.

He covered the distance to the old hand-made brick dwelling in long loping strides which Nerida could not match, and so she arrived behind him, almost at a run.

The wooden door with its rattling round metal knob opened easily, and inside the light was reasonably good, as the windows, although small, were uncurtained. The sagging wooden floorboards of the low-roofed verandah were repeated inside, and what was more, they were very dusty.

Nerida sneezed convulsively several times and Leigh pulled a clean white handkerchief from the back pocket of his jeans and silently handed it to her.

To the right of the corridor which they had first entered was a small lounge-room. At least, Nerida assumed that it would have been a lounge-room. There was a fireplace, some old armchairs, and a mattress on a high iron bed, but most of the space was filled with dusty hessian bags of flour, grain and other items.

Beyond the lounge was a kitchen containing a cast-iron wood-burning stove, a worn wooden bench and some rough shelves and cupboards. Leigh looked at the shelves and opened the cupboard doors impatiently, while Nerida unfastened the two windows and opened them wide. Anything to dissipate the suffocating dust and staleness!

'Crockery, cutlery, pots and pans. Two kerosene lamps, but no fuel. Candles, matches,' Leigh listed aloud. 'Salt, flour, quite a few tins of things—that's good. And this is a laundry through here. Broom and rags and cleaning equipment. Excellent!'

He took a brief look through a low doorway, then turned away, and Nerida poked her head in too. Two steps led down to a brick-floored room which contained an old-fashioned copper boiler and hand-turned mangle, as well as two large concrete sinks with taps above.

'Let's have a look at the bedrooms,' Leigh was saying, his boots already echoing along the wooden floor of the passage.

There were three—all small, all dusty, and all filled with an assortment of homestead stores piled neatly on one side to make way for iron bedsteads, heavy wadded mattresses and pillows.

'It'll have to do,' said Leigh.

Nerida nodded dumbly and again went to open the windows.

'It's not as bad as I feared, Nerida.'

'It isn't?'

'No. Obviously it's still used at times as stockmen's quarters. I thought there might have been windowpanes and floorboards missing, nothing in the kitchen at all, no bedding whatsoever. This way I'll have to bring sheets and blankets, fuel, a few other things, but that's all right.'

'Yes—well, in that case, it's a palace,' conceded Nerida drily.

'And it doesn't smell of mice.'

Nerida almost shivered with relief at this. She wasn't the type to jump on a chair screaming at the sight of one, but . . . is there anyone who really likes that scratching sound somewhere in the room at night, or the sight of a little grey tail disappearing behind the stove?

'Aha! And here's the reason why it doesn't,' Leigh added, turning at a sound in the passage. A black and white cat, looking independent, suspicious and half wild, ready to retreat at any moment, was rubbing itself around the edge of the back door, which was propped open with a brick. 'There are probably a couple of those here, specially to keep the mice down. Don't try to touch her, she'll be off like a shot.'

'She looks quite sleek. I hope she's keeping up with the population,' said Nerida.

'Let's look at the bathroom.' He moved and the cat disappeared immediately.

They went down the two back steps and saw it trotting out of sight around the corner of a shed out the back. The outside bathroom was, paradoxically, the most luxurious part of the house, having been added at a later date, and equipped with all modern conveniences, including a bore-water-fed shower and bath. There was no hot water, but Leigh explained that with the sun on the pipes and the already high temperature of the underground water, it was keeping it cool that could be a greater problem.

'But we should be unloading the boat. We can't waste any more time,' he added.

Nerida wiped down the kitchen bench with a cloth she found in the laundry and they simply dumped everything there, as it was the only clean spot. Things would have to be sorted out and unpacked properly later on.

'Coming back down to see me off before you start playing Cinderella?' Leigh drawled lazily after they had brought everything up.

'If you like,' Nerida nodded.

She was glad he had suggested it, although she didn't quite know why. It was not that she was reluctant to start the long chore of cleaning. They did not speak as they walked back to the dinghy, and Nerida had time to realise that her palms were wet and her heart was pounding, and it was not from exertion. He was about to step neatly into the little craft when impetuously, she stopped him with a hand on his arm, and forced him to meet her gaze.

'Will it be all right, Leigh?' The words came out thin and constricted from high in her throat, but her chin was lifted and her dark eyes were as steady as she could make them. He turned back to her slowly, as if pulled against his will.

'Yes, yes, it will,' he said. 'It has to be.'

He studied her silently for a moment, then reached out to her shoulders, gripping her slender form firmly, then running his hands down her arms and lacing his fingers through hers, squeezing them and caressing them.

She almost responded, but then he loosened the grasp and moved his hands to her face, cupping her chin in his smooth palms. She felt numb and uncertain, wanted simply to fall against the firm support of his chest and feel the beat of his heart and the rise and fall of his breathing against her cheek, but found she could not move. Then she saw—or felt—him stiffen and retreat, and his bright eyes narrowed and slid away to focus on the horizon.

'See you in a while,' he said through thin lips, and a moment later he was into the dinghy and away, using one oar like a punt-pole to force the boat as quickly as possible into deeper water.

CHAPTER SEVEN

NERIDA stood there for quite a long time after Leigh had gone, and thought she had never been so alone in all her life. His figure was tiny now, and the boat that supported him pitifully small. The current was carrying him further and further downstream, but he was making headway across, at least. He had explained that, again, he would not fight the water, but would go with it until he reached the other side where the current was far less, and where there might even be a slow reverse eddy which would help him back upstream to the homestead where the others waited.

The others . . . Shocked at herself, Nerida realised that she had been thinking only of Leigh, watching his progress impotently when she should already be up at the old house, preparing a clean room and bed for Margaret and making the rest of the place habitable for all of them as quickly as she could. If Leigh noticed that she was still standing here he would be furious. He wouldn't thank her for being so concerned for him.

Quickly she hurried up the slope to the lonely dwelling and began to work at a crazy pace, beating and turning the mattress in the largest bedroom, dusting every surface, sweeping and mopping the floor . . .

She brought in a rickety table from another bedroom and chocked its legs so that they were even, then laid out on it a few things that Margaret might need. There was still so much to bring over from the other homestead if ill Sam, injured Joe, frail Sandy and pregnant Margaret were to have the facilities and comfort they needed —blankets, sheets, pillows, towels, some toys and books to stave off the nightmare boredom that could lead to anxiety and tension if they had to stay here for long. More food, kerosene, a little spare clothing . . .

Nerida's mind buzzed ceaselessly with questions, plans and decisions as she worked on the second bedroom, and she realised that this was how Leigh must be feeling the whole time, since the responsibility for all of them rested so heavily on his shoulders.

She lost all track of time, forgot the fear and desperate aloneness that had clutched at her heart earlier, and was thus actually taken by surprise at the sound of Lucy's voice floating up from the thin tree mooring through the open windows.

'Neddie! Neddie! We're here. You have to come and help Mum.' She had arrived already, thumping on to the wooden verandah in her scuffed sneakers, panting and breathless.

Nerida quickly put down her mop and bucket—she had nearly finished this task now—and had just a few seconds in which to register with a faint smile that Lucy had adopted Sam's nickname now too, before the lively eight-year-old spoke again.

'It's Baby Karen again, and it's badder this time.'

'Is it? Right . . .' Nerida nodded, not betraying the alarm she felt at Lucy's words, as she followed the T-shirt and jeans-clad child down to the boat. Of course little Lucy didn't really understand the gravity of the situation, but Nerida and Leigh had both feared that this would happen—that the strain and anxiety and discomfort of the journey would start the dangerously premature pains again.

One look at Leigh's strained face and Margaret's contorted one told her that Lucy had not been exaggerating—the pains were indeed 'badder'. Margaret was crouching awkwardly in the bottom of the boat, half sitting, half lying, and there were beads of sweat covering her face and neck.

Leigh had lifted little Sam out of the dinghy and he stood beside Ross, crying dryly. Nerida scooped him on to her hip and rocked him soothingly.

'Nothing to cry about, Sammy love, Neddie's here,' she said, and then improvised a rash promise. 'You're going to have a lovely drink soon, too.'

Surprisingly, he did quieten quite quickly. He probably was thirsty after the sunny journey.

'Sheets and blankets for Margaret's bed, and some things for lunch,' Leigh said tersely, swinging two plastic bags towards her. She grasped them awkwardly and then placed Sam on the ground again.

'Go with Lucy and Ross, Sam,' she ordered. The three children set off.

'Can you stand up, Margaret?' Leigh questioned urgently.

'Yes, I'm all right again now.'

'How far apart are the pains?' asked Nerida.

'About ten minutes,' Margaret told her.

'But irregular,' Leigh put in. 'She's had three while we've been in the boat . . . Gently does it.'

He was out of the dinghy, bending down towards Margaret and giving her as much support as he could. When she was safely on her feet she stood between Leigh and Nerida leaning heavily on both of them.

'We'll just take it very, very slowly and gently,' said Leigh. 'Breathe deeply and calmly, and as soon as you want to stop, just say so.'

It took ten minutes for them to reach the house, and just as they stepped on to the verandah Margaret was gripped by another spasm of pain. Leigh guided her to the lumpy bed in the lounge, while Nerida went with feverish haste to make up the bed in the largest room with the sheets Leigh had brought.

Automatically she registered that the children seemed safely occupied. They had found the black and white cat and were trying in vain to coax it from its refuge beneath an old low-slung dray out the back. She had time, also, to wonder about old Sandy and shy Joe alone back at the new homestead.

Would Leigh stay here with Margaret? What if it became apparent that her delivery was imminent? At least this room was now clean and smelled fresh. She had found a clean canvas tarpaulin and had thrown it over the stored bags of supplies—this room seemed to contain mainly cement. She had even given the window-panes a quick dry wipe to remove most of the dust cleanly and without smearing. In the bathroom she had noticed pine-scented disinfectant and had added it to her mopping water to leave a tang in the air as well as killing bacteria.

As soon as the room was ready she called Leigh and he helped Margaret into the bed.

'How's that?'

'Lovely. Much better,' Margaret nodded. 'You've done wonders, Nerida. I can imagine what this place looked like before you started.'

The tone was artificially cheerful and they could both tell that Margaret was terrified for the baby.

'Just lie quietly and Nerida will bring you a hot drink as soon as she's able,' Leigh told her, retreating from the room and signalling with a subtle hand on Nerida's waist that she should follow him.

They went to the kitchen and Leigh began, as he spoke, to lay a fire expertly in the stove, using news-paper, kindling wood and small chopped gum logs from a woodbox next to it.

'What are we going to do?' asked Nerida, then bit her lip.

He had challenged this attitude of hers before, as she well remembered, and yet she just could not help looking to him for answers. He was clearly so capable of finding them. Nervously she sought out his eyes, and saw that his expression was indeed very distant, but he answered her question without commenting on it.

'I have to get back to pick up Sandy and Joe,' he said tersely. 'Even if the worst does happen and her labour won't stop, the birth should be some hours off yet. I'll check her dilation in a minute to make sure.'

'You won't want me for that,' said Nerida, trying to regain lost ground by sounding as efficient as she could. Why were there these bouts of distance and coldness from him today? Was it just his preoccupation with all that he had to do? Or did she somehow keep losing the respect and warmth she felt she had won from him by the end of yesterday? 'So I'll give the children a drink and a snack—if I can find one.'

'I brought biscuits.'

'And I'll get a kettle boiling as quickly as I can.'

'Good. See you in a few minutes, then.'

He left abruptly, without another word, and Nerida turned to the stove to light it with the matches he had thrust roughly into her hand. For several seconds her fingers shook and she struck the box feebly, producing not even a spark, then at last she created a flickering flame and cupped it in her hand as she lit the twists of paper. She rinsed out the kettle and put it on the stove, found a packet of tea in a cupboard, and—amazingly—some lime juice cordial which looked and smelt quite useable. Sam would have his 'lovely drink' after all.

The children had received their snacks and gone outside to enjoy them in the sunshine, and the kettle was beginning to sing when Leigh returned.

'Only four centimetres,' he said. 'And that's quite normal for someone who's already had two pregnancies. I'm off.'

'Leigh . . .' Nerida began, but he had already gone. She didn't know what she had intended to say, anyway.

It was funny that she immediately felt the return of the intense solitude she had known earlier, although she had four human souls around her now. Perhaps when the tea was made she could chat with Margaret as they drank it. It would help to take her mind off the pains, and that was more important than tackling the cleaning that still needed to be done.

It would also take Nerida's own mind off her insistent and discomfiting thoughts of Leigh and his increasingly unaccountable effect on her mood and senses . . .

Chatting did seem to help Margaret emotionally, but unfortunately not physically. When Nerida asked after half an hour if the pains, still coming irregularly every ten to twenty minutes, were easier, it was only the pregnant woman's optimism and brave front which made her nod and smile.

'Yes, definitely weaker.'

Nerida confronted Leigh with the news as soon as he returned, an hour and a half after setting off, with Sandy and Joe. He frowned and said nothing, simply passing her some gear from the boat, then turning to help Sandy out and shoulder Joe for another piggyback ride.

The poor old man was very dazed and dopey after the tranquilliser he had been given, and the strange unexplainable journey he had just been taken on, and made very slow, wandery progress up the hill. Nerida could see that Leigh was gritting his teeth in impatience, not because he had no sympathy for the time-worn old drover, but simply because there was so much still to do and to worry about, and activity was an antidote to anxiety in these circumstances.

'I'm going to start giving her some steroid injections,' he decided when they were almost at the homestead.

'Then you're fairly sure that . . .' Nerida began.

'I'm not sure of anything,' he ground out. 'I damn well know what I hope, though, and that's that it doesn't happen, but if it does . . .'

'At thirty-three weeks, though . . .'

'Unless she's in hospital the baby doesn't have a chance,' he agreed abruptly, cutting off her words. 'But if somehow we're out of here safely within the next twenty-four hours, and she's had those steroids to develop the baby's lungs ready for a hospital birth, then we've done all we can. How's the cleaning going?'

'Well, I spent a while with Margaret,' Nerida said reluctantly. 'And I've got lunch ready, which took a while because Sam was very distracting.'

She found she was frightened of his disapproval of the way she had spent the time, and knew that her tone was meek and defensive, but he wasn't angry as she had half expected.

'Fine. We'll eat as soon as I've checked Margaret and

given her the first injection, and then I'll be off again.'

'You must be exhausted, Leigh,' she blurted without thinking.

'I will be by the end of the day.' A frank, surprising grin accompanied the words.

'This is Jerilda!' old Sandy suddenly exclaimed as they stepped on to the verandah, looking about him with a brief flash of alertness. 'We've come to good old Jerilda. Good old Jerilda!'

Then he began to mumble, with vague pleasure in his eyes. Nerida and Leigh exchanged a relieved look. If Sandy had happy memories of this place then he was far less likely to become agitated and difficult.

Margaret seemed pleased about the steroid injections —it was fortunate that they had been in one of the boxes Leigh had already brought over—and she became more relaxed straight away. It was the lay person's faith in modern medical techniques, Nerida knew. Margaret did not fully grasp that the injections would neither stop her labour nor enable the baby to survive at this stage outside of a humidicrib, but if she was calmed and reassured by the treatment, then that was an achievement in itself.

'She's no further dilated,' said Leigh, after making another examination. 'That's something, at least.'

He bolted a quick meal of biscuits and cheese and tinned salads, then gulped down an enamel mug of water and was off again. As before, Nerida was shocked at the strength of her reaction over his departure. Was it just her fear that the deadly roar of the approaching flood-crest would begin to sound when he was trapped in the boat in the very centre of the channel? Fear for the safety of the man they were all relying on? Or was it something more?

Over two hours later she was reading a story to Joe and Sam in the third bedroom she had cleaned out, when Lucy and Ross scampered in to announce 'Leigh's back!' And the relief that flooded her and the thankfulness that sang in her heart as she sprang to her feet, abandoned

the story and went down to meet him told her quite
clearly that something was happening.

'I'm starting to need him as a man, not as a doctor,'
she realised. To need the sight of those capable arms and
steady blue eyes, to need the sound of warmth in his
voice or a laugh in his throat—far more than she needed
his knowledge, his expertise, and his decisiveness. And
heaven knew, she needed those things badly enough
too!

How could this be happening? How long had she
known him? Two days? It was ridiculous!

As she approached the boat she could see that he was
nearing exhaustion. He was swinging a bag of food tins
on to the ground when she arrived and he had not seen or
heard her. For several seconds he just stood there,
leaning over the bag and panting, his hands trembling
with fatigue. His temples, neck, shirt were all damp with
sweat.

'What about some coffee, Leigh? I'll put the kettle on
straight away.'

He straightened immediately, taken by surprise, and
she saw him sway a little before he mastered the dizzi-
ness that had gripped him momentarily.

'I'll have some water,' he said. 'No time to wait for the
kettle if I'm to be back before dark. How's Margaret?'

'The last contraction was nearly three-quarters of an
hour ago. When I looked in on her a few minutes ago,
she seemed to be asleep.' It was wonderful to be able to
give him this good news, and she studied his face keenly
for a reaction.

'Good!' For a moment his whole expression softened
and relaxed. It showed relief and pleasure, but it also
gave away his weariness. Impulsively, Nerida took a step
towards him.

'Leigh, you can't row all that way back again! I won't
let you,' she said passionately. 'You must have barely
slept last night and . . . show me your hands!'

It was a swift pulse of intuition that made her add this.
Leigh shook his head, but she grabbed at them and held

them with her slim fingers, turning the palms upwards. They were blistered and torn and red from pulling again and again at the rough splintery wood of the old oars.

'How would it be if you had to deliver Margaret's baby with hands like these?' she demanded.

'I'd manage,' he said lightly, but she heard his quick intake of breath as she touched the spot where a splinter lay beneath throbbing flesh. Her own skin tingled at the contact and closeness to him, but she willed herself to ignore this.

'You can't make another trip,' she repeated, still holding his sore hands.

'I have to,' he insisted. 'We've got no fresh food. I want to raid the Winthrops' vegetable garden. Margaret and the children have no spare clothes over here yet. We still need more blankets, and books and toys if we can fit them in. And I want to paint a sign on the roof to let them know we're here. On both roofs, there and here, so I want to bring the paint back . . .'

'Then I'll come with you,' said Nerida quickly. 'I can help with all that, and I'll row. Perhaps I could even go alone and you could stay here.'

'No, Nerida. Don't be silly.'

'It's not . . .' she began.

'It is. Don't waste my time, please.' Leigh's tone was wearily cold and distant all of a sudden, and he had snatched his hands away from her gentle fingers.

'You don't seem to have much faith in my abilities,' she said thinly, picking up the bag of food tins, then following him as he shouldered a heavy box of medical gear in grim silence and began to make his way up the hill. 'I've done a little bit of rowing.'

'What, on one of your tame English rivers?' It was derisive, and she hated him coldly in that moment.

'Yes, on one of our tame English rivers,' she returned icily. 'But it does mean I know how to handle a pair of oars. I won't let them slip through the rowlocks after three pulls.'

He did not reply until they had reached the verandah

of the homestead and he had put the gear down with a grunt. 'All right then, if Margaret's pains really have stopped and she feels happy about being left alone, we'll both go, and you'll do some rowing.'

'Let me dress those hands first, too . . .'

'No time. Later, when we get back.'

Margaret accepted the idea with her usual stoicism after Leigh had questioned her closely about her condition and examined her again. Lucy was reassuring too.

'I can handle things here,' she nodded confidently. 'I've already got Sandy splitting kindling. That's his job at our place, you see. And I finished reading the story for Joe and Sam. Joe says his foot's fine, and I think the swelling's going down.'

'I think you should seriously consider becoming a nurse, Lucy,' Leigh said solemnly to the freckled live-wire.

'Oh, yes, I decided that myself yesterday,' she said airily. 'Even a doctor, maybe. I want to do operations on people.'

'Well, I'll leave everything in your hands then, Dr Kelly.'

'Good! Can Ross be my assistant? And can I give the patient another injection?'

'No fear!' Margaret put in decisively, dampening the enthusiasm of the brilliant junior surgeon somewhat.

Leigh and Nerida made their escape under the cover of Lucy's disappointed protestations, and Nerida was relieved to notice that the real doctor's mood had lightened a little under the influence of the aspiring doctor's precocious words.

'Will you continue with the steroid injections?' she asked him when they were on their way down to the boat.

'For the moment.'

'For the moment?' she queried.

'Rather imprecise, I know. But we're dealing with so many unknown quantities.'

'Yes . . .'

Nerida took her place between the oars in the bows of the dinghy, and caught Leigh's cool silent regard. He was still standing on the bank, and she saw that he was unbuttoning his damp blue shirt. It was after four and the sun was no longer overhead, but it was still quite warm. Deliberately, still meeting her gaze, he peeled off the garment and threw it casually into the bottom of the boat, then held out a hand to Nerida.

'Stand up,' he said.

'You said I was . . .'

'Not this first bit. It'd be idiotic. I can handle the current easily—I've had the practice!—and get us across safely. That's not the part that's tough on my hands. You can row us upstream, which *is* hard, and then I'll guide us back. Fair enough?'

'OK.' She moved to the stern of the boat and sat facing the way they would be travelling.

It was a relief to be able to turn from him and study the scenery. It had been hard not to be aware of his broad tanned chest with its sculpted muscles and even patch of dark hair, and of his firm shoulders with their scattering of darker freckles.

They did not speak at all. Nerida felt uncomfortable about the silence, but she would have felt worse about breaking it. Even when they reached the other side —uneventfully—and changed positions so that she could row, Leigh said only one word, 'Oops!' as the boat rocked unsteadily and he was forced to hold her waist for a few moments with both hands to regain his equilibrium.

Rowing was harder than Nerida had expected, and she had not made the mistake of expecting it to be easy. The boat was heavy and old, and the oars were a little warped, as well as being rough on the hands. Nerida knew that her own palms, more tender than Leigh's, would be blistered before they arrived at the new home-stead, but she gritted her teeth and carried on steadily, suppressing instinctive grunts of effort, but knowing that her face was stretched into a grimace at each pull.

Leigh did not look at her, but kept his eyes fixed beyond her on what lay ahead, ready to warn her of obstacles. And, like her, he was always listening, sometimes consciously, sometimes quite unconsciously, for the roar of the flood-crest in the gorge that might begin at any time, unlikely though it seemed in this glorious fine weather.

When they finally stepped on to the verandah of the new homestead, Nerida took in deep gulps of air and felt a great load lift from her shoulders, although she was still shaking with fatigue.

'He must feel, now, that I'm not just a dead weight in this crisis,' she thought. Surely the barriers he put up between them, the coldness that emanated from him, the terseness in his voice when he spoke to her, would all disappear for good now, and she would experience many more of those moments of oneness that had been so sweet and so rare!

But no.

'Good work,' was all he said. 'I didn't think you'd do it.'

And for a second one arm lay across her shoulders and squeezed them, but it was gone again and he had moved well away from her, as if deliberately shaking off the body contact, before she could react to the fact that it was there. Nerida was angry.

'Well, you were wrong, weren't you!' she spat out crisply.

'Yes.'

'It's probably a very salutary experience for you, I imagine.'

'I dare say it is.' The words were absent and she realised that her barbs had not even grazed the surface.

She felt petty for letting him get to her like this, and tossed her fair head to try to shake off the feeling physically. Damn him! Damn him for being able to swing her from happiness to humiliation in a matter of moments! Her hands were throbbing, but she was less aware of that than of the intangible emotional pain inside her.

The homestead seemed strangely deserted after the life it had contained last night and this morning. Leigh had already tidied and rearranged most of the cool airy rooms, and they wasted no time wandering about, but began to load the boat up straight away.

After they had put in everything needed from the house, Leigh led the way to the back, where there were several plots of vegetable garden, all of it now under at least two inches of sluggish water. They found winter lettuce, spinach, carrots, and nearly a dozen decent-sized potatoes. It wasn't a feast of fat things, but it would go a long way towards relieving the boredom and improving the nutritional value of an otherwise canned and packaged diet.

'Now for the painting,' said Leigh when they had collected an adequate supply of things for several days.

He moved the ladder to the roof of the main house and took up the opened paint can and two brushes. Nerida followed him. Another test for her nerves and spirit. She wasn't particularly fond of ladders. The paint was olive green, not the most vibrant of colours for the job, but the only choice they had.

'We'll paint a rough circle,' said Leigh, 'with an arrow inside it pointing in the direction of the old homestead.'

He was painting the rough outline of it as he spoke, slopping the stuff on quickly and carelessly. Nerida began filling it in straight away, because having something to do helped her to forget that she felt as if she might slide off this roof at any moment.

The brushes were thick and they completed the job quite quickly, but the light was growing golden now as the sun sank lower, so they did not have much time to spare before dark.

It felt funny to be abandoning the pleasant, well-furnished rooms of the new homestead to their fate. As they took a last look through the house to make sure that nothing of importance had been left behind, Nerida tried to picture it as it would look after the crest had passed through.

The floor might be inches deep in silt and debris in parts, according to what Leigh had told her, the walls would be stained and smeared, and broken objects would be flung against each other in derelict heaps. It would be heartbreaking work to put it all to rights again, but there was nothing they could do to save the house. As much as possible had already been piled out of reach.

'You'd think they would have moved more things over to the old homestead,' Nerida remarked as they shut the front door for the last time.

'They didn't realise the extent of the danger until it was too late,' Leigh replied. 'Even the old-timers were taken by surprise. It's the localised storms closer to home coming on top of the heavy rains further to the east that have compounded the whole mess, and created the danger of this crest we're still expecting.'

The crest . . . In spite of the ever-present danger, Nerida could not help enjoying the last boat trip downstream. Leigh was an expert now at coaxing the boat across while still running with the current, and the flooded desert landscape was at its most beautiful at this time of day. The water was a gold mirror, reflecting the stately white arms of the trees; flocks of birds wheeled about noisily, getting ready to settle for the night; and the rough rock of the cliffs opposite glowed with colour that changed and deepened every minute. Nerida saw kangaroos—some with dusty orange backs, and others with purplish-grey ones—coming quietly down to the water's edge for their evening drink, and was lulled by the patterned croaking of frogs.

'If I shut my eyes I'd be able to imagine this was a gondola and we were in Venice,' she said with a smile, catching Leigh studying her momentarily and wondering what it meant. 'Only it's too beautiful to shut them, so I'm keeping them wide open.'

'Yes, you were so quiet I thought you might be dozing.' So that was what it meant. Only that. What had she been expecting? His torso was still bare, and his skin glowed with health. Quickly she turned away.

'Do you realise that we're safe now?' Leigh said as he tied up the boat for the last time. 'We're all safely out of reach of the flood-crest, and we've got food and clothes and water and shelter.'

She could hear the satisfaction in his voice and sensed the sudden temporary draining of a tension that had been gripping him ever since she had known him. She wanted to respond to his exultant mood, take advantage of it in some way while it lasted, but she did not know how, could not find the right words which would show that she shared his feelings.

'We'll unload,' he went on. 'Then perhaps you could rustle up something for dinner while I drag the dinghy further up the slope—not that the old tub's really worth the effort, but it's better that it doesn't get washed downstream, as we may turn out to need it again.'

'Sounds sensible to me,' agreed Nerida in a cheerful tone. At least she could always talk to him in a reasonable way when it came to practical matters.

When they arrived at the homestead the fire was lit in the lounge and everyone was grouped around it, including Margaret, who was reclined on the old bed that Leigh intended to use that night. She looked guilty when they came in and said immediately, 'I had to get up to go to the bathroom, so I thought I might as well come and lie in here where it's cosy and cheerful. I haven't had any more pains.'

'Then you're forgiven,' Leigh told her. 'But if you need to move again, best to let me carry you.'

Two hours later Nerida had served a quite passable meal of tinned spaghetti bolognaise, vermicelli and salad. It had felt almost like pioneering, using the solid old saucepans on the iron range, and working by the light of a single kerosene lamp. Strangely heart-warming and satisfying, especially with the sound of the children's lazy chatter in the other room.

Sam had been grizzly and feverish again, and did not

eat much, but that was only to be expected. He quietened after the meal was cleared away, and Nerida was soon pleased to see from her own lazy position, sipping tea on a blanket on the floor near the hearth, that he had dropped off to sleep. Lucy and Ross had too, as they had been playing energetically outside all afternoon.

Leigh leaned towards her from the old armchair he had flung himself into.

'Time for some splinter surgery, I think, Nerida,' he said cheerfully. 'Let's have a look at those hands.'

'Only a couple.' She held out her hands and felt a weakening thrill of awareness course through her at his touch.

'That's a nasty one, though,' he mused, pressing one tender spot gently with the ball of his thumb.

'Ouch! Yes!' I must fight this, Nerida thought feverishly.

Her palms were painful to the touch, and the splinter he had pressed had pricked sharply beneath the skin, yet her awareness of his warm touch and of his torso bending towards her was far stronger than the sensation of pain. His blue shirt, which had been rinsed out, was draped to dry near the fire, and he wore only the black pullover above his jeans, its sleeves rolled casually to the elbows and its V neck revealing the tan that had deepened during the day in spite of the protective sunburn cream he had applied earlier in the afternoon.

He was on his feet now and had gone to the laundry where they had stored most of the medical equipment they had brought. He returned a moment later with tweezers, antiseptic, cotton wool, soothing cream and Band-Aid—a simple collection of surgical items indeed!

'You first?' he asked laconically.

'OK,' nodded Nerida.

He set to work on the most difficult first. It was a ridiculously simple procedure, one that would normally be vastly beneath many a doctor's dignity, but Nerida felt that she had glimpsed a part of Leigh Russell the doctor, as opposed to Leigh Russell the man, that she had not seen before.

His fingers were quite steady as he held the small pair of tweezers, and his concentration was as focused as if he had been performing major surgery in an operating theatre. She saw that he did not simply plunge in, but took a good look at the dark length of wood and its surrounding tender red flesh before he positioned the tweezers.

When he did pinch them together on her flesh, he grasped the splinter at first try and drew it gently and firmly out, causing as little pain and discomfort as he could and leaving nothing behind beneath the skin.

And now that he had finished, he was immediately cheerful and relaxed:

'There! That's one. The other two should be much easier.'

They were, and he was finished only a moment later. She didn't even need a Band-Aid. A little cream would soften and soothe the skin and in a day or two her palms would be as smooth as they had ever been.

'My turn,' he said now, sterilising the tweezers again quickly in the fire.

'I must warn you, I'm expecting you to make a terrible patient,' Nerida said lightly, to hide a slight nervousness. 'Doctors always do.'

His hands were in a far worse condition than hers had been, and his nearness made her fingers less steady and her concentration less direct than it normally was.

'I'll close my eyes and think about other things,' he promised.

'Thank you.' She looked carefully at his hands and then began to use the tweezers as delicately as she could.

'You must make an excellent nurse when it comes to real medicine,' he remarked after several moments, his eyes still faithfully closed. What long, thick lashes he had! It was the first time she had noticed it.

'I was just thinking the same about you,' she said quickly, to quell this sudden awareness, and an even worse desire to run her fingers or her lips softly over his face in tender exploration.

'Thank you,' was his reply.

It was a relief when she had finished. His eyes were still closed.

'Those thoughts must be pretty interesting,' Nerida said teasingly. His eyes snapped open, startling her for the hundredth time with their blueness in his tanned face, and he smiled.

'Oh, my thoughts? Yes, they were. Very interesting.' It was an unreadable smile.

'I'll put everything away.' Nerida got hurriedly to her feet.

'And I'll carry the kids off to bed.'

Nerida saw that Joe was asleep now too. She took up her seat near the fire again and sprawled there, enjoying the crackling warmth that toasted her limbs. Soon she ought to go to bed too, but why not lie here for a little longer?

Sandy suddenly started to sing as he gazed into the shimmering-bright coals of the fire. He had an old man's weak and slightly quavery voice, but it was low and surprisingly tuneful, and the songs he sang were old Australian bush ballads about the things that he himself had known—droving and shearing—that had a haunting quality out here in this desert homestead, with only the orange light of the fire, the smoky yellow of the kerosene lamps and the tangy smell of burning gum logs.

'There's a trade we all know well,
It's bringing cattle over,
On every track to the Gulf and back,
They know the Queensland drover.

Pass the billy round, boys,
Don't let the pint pot stand there,
For tonight we'll drink the health
Of every overlander.'

Two verses later, Nerida was asleep.

Her next dim awareness was of being scooped up by two strong arms and carried out of the warm room. Her face was pressed into a soft woolly surface that smelt musky, smoky and somehow familiar. It was Leigh, of course. Still three-quarters asleep, this realisation only made her burrow more closely into his chest and let out a soft sighing sound when his arms tightened around her.

It seemed quite natural, too, when his warm firm lips began to kiss her closed eyes gently, then moved down to find her mouth, caressing it slowly and expertly into a response. When he laid her down on the cold and rather rough woollen blanket that covered her bed, it was partly the sleepy instinct for warmth and comfort that made her arms slide around his neck to pull him down after her. She wanted to keep hold of his strong, delicious body, to keep those lips exploring hers, to lose her fingers in a tangle of his hair, and feel her own blonde curls brush across his face and be caressed away again.

She was about to murmur his name, wanting to roll it on her tongue like a sweet morsel, and see how it felt to whisper that syllable with tenderness into his ear, but just as she took her lips softly away from his kiss to do so, he stiffened and rolled off the bed and on to his feet in one lightning-fast movement. It was an unmistakable gesture of rejection.

He did not leave at once, though, and Nerida could sense through her closed lids that he was staring down at her. What she could not sense, of course, was his expression. One thing was clear: he was already regretting the impulse, whatever it had been, that had led him to kiss her, and Nerida felt humiliated by her own nakedly willing response.

If she could just pretend that she was asleep—although sleep felt miles away now—then he might believe that her caresses had been so instinctive as to be meaningless. Perhaps he would think that she had been dreaming of someone else. Should she murmur another name, as if in sleep? No, that would be going too far. But she would roll over with eyes still closed and bury her face in the pillow, he would believe that she slept still and would go.

He did, only a moment later, shutting the wooden door behind him with a quiet but definite click, and Nerida was left alone on her bed, with the chill of the room striking down on her. For a few minutes she waited tensely to make sure that he was really gone and had no intention of returning; then she stripped off her outer garments stiffly and crawled beneath the sheets in bra and pants.

CHAPTER EIGHT

SAM woke her in the night with his feverish cries. Nerida got out of bed reluctantly, knowing that there was some reason why she did not want to wake up properly and start thinking about things. It came as she pulled the top blanket off her bed and wrapped it round herself— Leigh, and their kiss. Her heart plummeted and she felt almost sick.

It was only now that she realised how much her attraction to him had grown during the day. There had been so much else to think about and do, and yet they had been thrust so closely together by these circumstances. It was completely unlike a normal meeting between a man and a woman. Usually you had time and distance to give some perspective. When you first met a man, you didn't suddenly start spending almost twenty-four hours a day in his company, with life-and-death problems to resolve together . . .

But it was Sam who needed her attention now, not Leigh or her unsettling relationship with him. She took the little boy's temperature and found that it was the highest it had been. Probably it would be tonight that the fever would break. Tomorrow his spots would come and he would be a much happier child.

At the moment, though, he was sticky with sweat, which must be stinging to the chafed patches of eczema on his little body. Nerida crept out of the room, not wanting to wake anyone—especially Leigh—in search of some warm water to sponge him a little, as well as the aspirin from one of the medical chests.

Leigh had said that the underground water that came out through the bathroom taps was already hot, but she also knew by this time that it was full of harsh mineral salts which would do more harm than good to Sam's

135

sensitive skin. There was nothing for it but to go to the kitchen, where the water came from a rainwater tank outside, and heat some in the kettle.

Leigh, a humped figure in a grey blanket, did not stir as she tiptoed through the moon-brightened room, but she winced at the metallic splash of water thudding into the kettle. That would be bound to wake him. And of course the kitchen stove was quite cold by this time. She would either have to set a new fire and light it, or use the still-glowing coals of the lounge-room fire. It would have to be the latter. She couldn't go to all the trouble of lighting the kitchen fire just to avoid being in the room with Leigh!

He rolled over and woke up as she was crouched in front of the hearth, blowing gently on the coals to bring them to life again.

'What's up?' he asked in a voice that was rusty from sleep. He sat up slightly, and his hair was tousled like a boy's.

'It's Sam. He's very feverish and sticky.' Nerida realised that the blanket around her had slipped open and that she was very inadequately clad beneath it. Hastily she pulled the wool more closely around her, took a steadying breath and went on, 'I'm heating up some water to sponge him down, and I'll give him half an aspirin, then sit up with him till he goes back to sleep.'

'Right,' Leigh nodded briefly, then simply rolled over and tucked his chin down into the bedding, as if her presence was of less than no interest to him.

Nerida felt that her action with the blanket had irritated him with its prudishness, and she burned with humiliation as she waited for the water to warm. Leigh made no further movement or sound. Was he asleep? She doubted it. He was simply ignoring her.

Her bed was very cold when she crept back into it after Sam had settled at last, and it seemed to take her a long time to warm up and relax enough to sleep. The sun streamed brightly into the room the next morning when she awoke again, and she knew that it must be late. After

his feverish, broken night, Sam was still sleeping peace-
fully. Nerida saw that the spots had come out on his face
and hands, and that his hair was no longer lying in
tendrils dampened by sweat. It was a good sign, and
there was no point in waking him.

She dressed quietly and quickly, listening to the
sounds coming from the rest of the house. Lucy and Ross
were up, and Margaret was awake. The three were
talking together in their room. Leigh must be up too, but
she could not hear his voice or footsteps.

This would be a strange day, a day of waiting, and she
dreaded it suddenly. If nothing happened—no flood-
crest, no rescue—would she and Leigh have hours to
spend together with none of the preoccupations they had
shared until now, preoccupations that had always served
to deflect tension and awareness?

She hoped that there would be a way of avoiding him.
Perhaps rescue *would* come this morning, or if it didn't,
she could spend the day with Margaret, and with Joe and
Sam.

'Oh, you're awake.' Lucy greeted her briskly as she
stepped out of her room and into the narrow passageway. 'I've got to fill you in on what's happening, Leigh
says. I'm the Director of Medical Administration
today.'

'And I'm her assistant,' added little Ross, wanting
some notice too.

'Are you? That's a very important job,' said Nerida,
gratifying him exceedingly.

'Let's go into the kitchen so you can have breakfast
while I explain,' said Lucy. 'Leigh—I mean, Dr Russell
—said you were treating a patient during the night.
That's why we let you sleep in.'

'That was nice of you,' said Nerida, keeping a straight
face with difficulty.

'There's eggs and baked beans for you in here,' Lucy
went on, ignoring her. 'The fire's still going. Pity there's
no bread.'

'I'm going to have a try at making some today,' Nerida

decided. She had found dried yeast in the pantry at the new homestead and had brought it over.

'Great! That'll be yummy!' Lucy exclaimed, and Ross agreed. 'Mummy's having breakfast in bed. Leigh's gone to get more firewood because this is the last of what we've got, in this box. Ross and me are going to take Sandy for a walk. Dr Russell informs me that he's very restless again this morning.'

'How come he's got Alp Climber's disease if he's always lived out here?' Ross put in. 'We don't have any alps.'

'Yes, I was wondering that too, Dr Kelly,' Lucy confessed. 'Perhaps Sister Palmer could explain to us.'

But Nerida could not. '*Alp Climber's* disease!' A moment later the truth dawned and she bubbled over helplessly with laughter.

'Sorry, kids,' she managed to gasp a minute later. If only Leigh was here to enjoy this! 'It's not Alp Climber's disease, it's Altzheimer's disease. That's just someone's name. It's an illness a lot of old people get, and it's not anything to do with having climbed too many mountains. Much less interesting, I know.'

'Could we catch it?' asked Ross, round-eyed.

'Sister Palmer just explained, Dr Kelly. You don't listen. You can only catch it if you're old.'

'You don't *catch* it, Lucy,' smiled Nerida. 'In fact, medical scientists aren't sure yet exactly what causes it. It might be diet, it might be hereditary—something you're more likely to get if your parents had it, it might be all sorts of things.'

'Anyway, we'd better go and find him before he wanders off,' said Lucy, having clearly had enough of this medical discussion. 'Pity Joey can't come with us. He's having his breakfast in bed too.'

The two children clattered off outside. It *was* a pity about Joe, Nerida thought as she put on water for coffee and cracked an egg into the heavy cast-iron frying-pan on the stove. Its yolk stayed unbroken, which was a good sign. These eggs had been rubbed with greasy egg-preserver, but if a patch of shell had got missed accidentally, the result could be nasty. Joe was a shy boy in these unaccustomed conditions, clearly much preferring to spend his time out in the bush, by the creek or amongst animals.

When Leigh returned, she would ask him if it would be possible to carry the aboriginal child somewhere closer to the rock cliffs, where he could lie on a rug in the shade of a tree and watch wild life and landscape. It would be much nicer for him than being cooped up in the house. And in fact right now he could easily be brought out on to the verandah, and she would sit with him while she ate her own breakfast.

The two didn't talk much, but Nerida sensed that he was content, and found that she was surprisingly so herself. It was such a glorious day. The swollen waters slipping inexorably past looked almost benign under the bright sun, and the birds that wheeled and chattered around the untidy leafy crowns of the gums gave life and colour and innocence to the scene. Faintly in the distance she could hear the rhythmic and almost melodic echo of an axe. It would be Leigh, chopping wood, and he would be back soon with his load.

Somehow this thought didn't strike up chords of confused feelings in her this morning, as it would have done last night. In the incredibly clear air of the outback morning, she could not regret their kiss, and found herself believing that his stiffening and rejection had been a mistake, a misunderstanding.

In a strange way it seemed so right to be sitting here with the sound of his axe in the distance. She could almost imagine that they were pioneers. Perhaps it would be nice one day to live that kind of life. Not completely, of course, and not in such a desert landscape. But to live in an old house with acres of land, fruit trees and vegetables and chickens. She might bake her own bread, and take up some old-time crafts, do nursing work part-time in a bush hospital. There would be a toddler or two playing in the back yard with a dog, and at the end of the day, Leigh would come home and——

She stopped the thoughts abruptly, and the optimistic mood vanished as suddenly and completely as it had come. Leigh's axe rang out twice more and then was silent, and the reality of his rejection of her came back with full force. It had been the seductive warmth of the fire that had created his need and impulse, and as soon as they were in her cold room, that need had vanished and left behind only his true feeling for her.

He would be at the homestead soon and she would have to face him again. She didn't want to. What was there to do to deflect the tension of their meeting?

Lots of things. The realisation came as a relief. She had already left Margaret alone for too long for a start. And she wanted to wash out Sam's nappies and everyone's spare garments, since each of them only had one change of clothing. Margaret might like a bath, and there was the bread to prepare. It needed to rise twice and be kneaded again before baking. Sam would soon be ready to be dressed and fed. Leigh had talked about painting a sign on this roof too . . .

A plane overhead, seeing the sign. Rescue. Nerida almost couldn't imagine it. Her world here was strangely self-contained, and in a way satisfying. Then a pang of remembrance shot through her. Somewhere under this bright bowl of blue sky Jim might by lying pinioned beneath the wreckage of his plane, lifeless, or, perhaps even worse, still living. There *was* a world outside, and it was a harsh one.

She scrambled to her feet and picked up mug and plate.

'Are you happy to stay out here, Joe love? Shall I bring you a book and some toys?'

'Nice out here,' Joe nodded. 'Watchin' the water. Book'd be nice too. 'N buildin' block toys.'

'I'll bring them out to you.'

He seemed more animated today, and she guessed that the injured foot was paining him much less, although Leigh was still giving him mild analgesics at intervals. She put her dirty dishes in the kitchen with the others—the dishes, another job to do!—then heard Sam crying insistently, and felt guilty and anxious about having left him for so long. Perhaps she'd been mistaken to conclude that he was much better today.

'Is that you, Nerida?' she heard Margaret call from her room.

'Yes, Margaret.'

'You've heard Sam, then. He's only just stirred, but I was worried because I knew I shouldn't get up.'

'No, that's right. You stay where you are. Do you need anything at the moment?'

'No, I'm fine, love, thanks.'

Nerida opened her bedroom door and found that nothing was really wrong. Sam had wanted to toddle out, but couldn't turn the rickety old door-handle. He brightened as soon as he saw her, and lifted up his little arms, wanting to be carried. Nerida swung him on to her hip. She had changed his makeshift nappy during the night and this one was still dry, which was good.

Soon he was washed and dressed and fed, and she tackled the dishes, using the undrinkable bore water that came hot and slightly acrid-smelling from one of the kitchen taps. Sam toddled about and needed an eye kept on him, so it was a slow job, made slower by the fact that she was waiting every moment for Leigh to appear. At this rate he'd be ready for morning tea by the time he arrived.

Then, unmistakably, she heard the sound of his axe ringing out again. How much wood was he planning to chop, for heaven's sake!

It was a while longer before the truth dawned. Nerida had made the dough for the bread, following the instructions on the packet of dried yeast and getting Sam to 'help' with stirring—a task that he had enjoyed greatly, but which had slowed down the process not a little. And Leigh was still chopping wood, the rhythmic sound a little fainter now, as if he had gone further upstream in search of more fallen trees and branches.

'He's deliberately avoiding me.' The realisation washed over her with the chill of iced water and she knew that she had found the right answer. Numbly, she continued to work, shocked as much by how hard it had hit her as by the rejection itself. 'I can't have come to feel like this about him so quickly. It can't just have crept up on me like that.'

But it had, and perhaps it was not so surprising. In a situation like this, did any of the usual rules apply at all?

Nerida found a large old metal dish, checked that it had no sharp edges or rust, and filled it with water. Then she sat it outside in the sun, made some paper boats out of old newspaper from the kitchen wood-box, and a paper sun-hat for Sam's head—which he thought hilarious—and sat him beside it in his little T-shirt and shorts, with protective block-out cream on his tender chafed skin. He played happily with the boats while she worked in the laundry, washing, rinsing and mangling the clothes.

She tried to compare her feelings for Leigh with what she had felt for Damon, but it just wasn't possible—a boy she had known almost as long as she could remember, versus a man who had entered her life only three days ago. A sedate, unchallenging and, let's face it, boring courtship, compared to something that wasn't a courtship at all, but was simply a few incidents, created only by emotions that were running high for other reasons entirely.

It was idiotic even to wonder if there was anything in it. Her relationship with Damon might have been doomed to wither from undernourishment, but this strange desert growth of feeling was like the wildflowers that grew here after rain—they sprang up quicker than you would believe possible, they glowed with an ephemeral beauty, and then they died and left the ground as bare and colourless as if they had never been.

Or it was like some perverse kind of holiday romance, so vivid while you were living it, and so foolish and feeble as soon as you returned to your real life.

Leigh had realised this, clearly, and had taken himself off this morning for far longer than was necessary, simply to signal with unequivocal directness that nothing further was to happen. It seemed to Nerida a rather crude way of doing it—just rolling over in bed blankly like that last night, and avoiding her this morning. She decided that a civilised agreement would have been better.

'He's not my type at all,' she said to herself firmly, pulling the last garment from the hand-turned mangle.

She piled the wet things in a plastic bucket she had found beneath the laundry sinks and went outside. No clothesline, of course, but she could rig something up between the house and the shed if she could find some rope or twine. Sam's boats were getting a little soggy, and he had probably spent long enough in the sun. She took him and his bowl to the front verandah, and he and Joe were soon absorbed in a game involving floating their building blocks in the water instead. It was delightful—for a moment, while she forgot Leigh—to see the aboriginal child's patience with Sam, and to see the two-year-old so much happier and less fretful this morning.

Nerida kneaded her dough again for its second rise, and found that there was actually some twine here in the kitchen on one of the upper shelves. Soon the washing was strung on a line in the sun, and it would be dry in next to no time.

'Would you like a bath, Margaret?' She had knocked on the pregnant woman's door, and gone in.

'Lovely—if you think I'll be all right. What does Leigh say?'

'He's not back yet.' Nerida said it lightly, but felt stupidly defensive, as if Margaret might be able to guess why it was that Leigh had stayed away for so long.

'He's probably got saddled with Sandy and the children,' chuckled Margaret.

'Yes, I'm sure that's it,' Nerida agreed without sincerity. 'But as for the bath, we'll take it gently and be very careful with your plaster too. You haven't had any pains since yesterday. I'm sure Leigh will think it's fine.'

Nerida filled the tub with hot bore-water and waited till it had cooled to the right temperature—which was a strange idea to get used to. It was a pity that the water was so harsh, but Margaret's skin was used to it after a lifetime spent in this region. The two women worked together in order to make the journey from the bed to the tub without putting any strain on Margaret's abdominal muscles, and she did not feel the least twinge of pain, which was an encouraging sign.

'This is marvellous. Something to do, and it feels so clean and soothing,' Margaret said when she had nearly finished, then, 'Isn't that Leigh?'

Nerida went outside to look. It was. He had a load of wood piled high in a rickety but still functional old pram, which had been the only wheeled thing he could find about the place.

When she saw him in his stockman's hat, and with shirt neck open and sleeves rolled to the elbows, Nerida felt a pang of nervousness, hurt and shame, but then she firmly took hold of herself. She simply could not afford to behave like a . . . like a what? a silly schoolgirl? something like that . . . with this man, when they two were the only able-bodied people responsible for six other human lives.

So she went resolutely to meet him, shivering momentarily in her pale grey blouse, although the sun struck warmly on her back.

'How's it going?' His expression was at once guarded, and his blue eyes were narrowed.

'Good,' she smiled automatically, and was glad that she could turn immediately and walk back with him to the homestead, because it meant that they were side by side and not face to face. Out of the corner of her eye she saw the semi-wild black and white cats scamper out of sight around the corner of the shed. 'I feel I've got quite a bit done this morning. Sam seems much happier. His spots are out and his fever's down, and he's playing with

Joe on the front verandah. I've started to make bread, and I've done the washing, as you can see . . .'

She was chattering, but it seemed the only way to re-establish a working relationship. It was Leigh who quickly found another way.

'You've got Margaret in the bath?' The words were snapped out aggressively.

They were at the back door, and Leigh suddenly stopped dead with the first two rough logs in his hand. He had been about to throw them on the ground to start a pile. Nerida had left the door of the outside bathroom open, and the bulk of Margaret's white body could just be seen in the blue enamel bathtub.

'Yes, I thought . . .' Nerida began, but he cut her off, his low voice throbbing with barely controlled anger. It took her completely by surprise, and the strength drained down through her legs and into the ground, leaving her fighting to control their trembling.

'This may be unlike any nursing work you've ever done before,' he said, 'but that gives you no cause to forget that our relationship is exactly the same as it would be in a major hospital. We're professionals, and out here we're professionals for twenty-fours hours a day. There are decisions that you're qualified to make, and other decisions that only I should be responsible for. I think you've forgotten that, and in future you'd better remember it.'

'Isn't it just as much that *you*'ve forgotten it?' Nerida broke out in low passionate tones.

On the surface, his outburst was about the fact that she had bathed Margaret without consulting him, but beneath this, they both knew that much more was on the agenda. It was last night's kiss, and the disturbing, fragile electricity that crackled between them, that was the real issue.

'Perhaps it is,' he conceded harshly. 'Perhaps that's why I'm talking about it now.'

'You've made your point, then,' said Nerida, lifting her chin so that the line of her jaw was clean and firm, and forcing herself to meet his so-cold gaze. 'We're professionals from now on, and frankly I wouldn't want it any other way. I'm sorry I gave Margaret a bath before consulting you. It won't happen again—nor anything like it.'

'Good. I'm glad. For lots of reasons.'

He bent and began to throw the gum logs into a pile with rhythmic, economical movements. The muscles of his back rippled beneath his shirt, and in spite of the fact that Nerida was still weak and shaken after the scene that had just taken place, she felt awareness course through her at the sight. Quickly she flicked her gaze away, and caught him wincing and flexing his hands.

'Leigh!' It was an involuntary exclamation. 'They're rubbed raw! You fool! Just because . . .'

She hastily bit back the next words. It would do no good to bring out into the open, to say aloud in blunt words, the reason for his obsessive work with the axe.

'We needed wood,' he shrugged. 'Are you suggesting Sandy should have done it? Or yourself? Your hands are blistered too.'

Nerida's fair hair blew across her face and she tucked it back. She did not know how to reply. In the silence between them, there was suddenly the faint and very distant thrum of an engine high in the sky. At first Nerida heard it only as a merciful release of the tension that still vibrated between them but Leigh's instant movement, his long strides covering the red ground, made her realise that it could mean much more than that.

She followed him quickly, then halted as he raced back into the house and emerged again seconds later with two blankets, one of which he flung at her.

'Run,' he ordered. 'Out into the open. Spread the blanket out and make as much movement with it as you can.'

The plane was almost overhead as they each began to dash crazily back and forth. It might have, it *must* have, looked weird, but there was no time to think of that.

Ross and Lucy were running and shouting in the distance.

'A plane! It's a plane!'

And even old Sandy's shuffling figure behind them seemed to be moving more quickly than usual. Nerida was exhausted and Leigh was breathless by the time they accepted that the plane had not changed its course, or descended, or started to circle back. No one had seen them. Probably this plane had not even been looking.

No one spoke as they returned to the house, except Sandy, who started talking about a cup of tea. The bathroom was empty when Nerida looked in, and she went quickly to Margaret's room. The pregnant woman was just climbing back on to her bed, made more awkwardly in her movements by the plaster on her arm.

'I feel fine,' she said a little defensively to Nerida. 'It seemed stupid just to go on lying in the bath waiting for you or Leigh. The plane didn't see us?'

'No.'

'Never mind, another one'll come along some time.' It was a piece of true outback philosophy, but it was said without Margaret's full quota of cheerfulness. There was an undercurrent of embarrassment in her manner, and Nerida knew that she had overheard the intense altercation at the woodpile, and felt uncomfortable because it had concerned her.

'Sandy wanted a cup of tea, so I'm going to put the kettle on,' Nerida told her lightly, deciding it was best not to refer to the whole wretched thing. 'Want one too?'

'That'd be lovely,' Margaret agreed, clearly relieved to be able to retreat to this safe subject. 'How's the bread?'

'Coming along fine last time I looked. Probably about time I kneaded it again and put it into loaf tins for the final rise.'

Nerida had already hunted out loaf tins from the cupboard, and oil to grease them with from the supplies she and Leigh had ferried over in their last trip yesterday. In the kitchen, the stove fire still had enough warmth to rekindle without using paper or matches, and the kettle was soon on. Lucy and Ross and Sandy had joined Sam and Joe on the verandah, and Nerida thought that Margaret would probably like to spend some time there this afternoon too.

Leigh had dumped the useless blankets back on his bed and had gone out to check on everyone, saving Margaret for last and shutting the door so that Nerida, from her position in the kitchen, could not hear what he said to her. Then his footsteps struck heavily on the wooden steps that led from the back door and he had grasped the handle of the old pram again, ready to go and collect more of the wood he had cut.

Unwillingly, Nerida watched him through the kitchen window as he set off, kicking at the rickety wheels when they caught on stones. As if he had felt the intensity of her gaze, he turned for a moment and their eyes met, but he gave no smile or sign of acknowledgement at all, and Nerida turned angrily away. Was this his idea of how 'professionals' worked together? She was glad she had never been on a hospital ward with him!

The bread dough thumped heavily on to the wooden bench as she kneaded it. She was probably crushing all those yeast organisms to death, but she didn't care. They could all eat leaden bread. She wanted to feel this anger against him, and she wanted to vent it, too. Slap! Twist . . . Slap! Twist . . . Leigh had taken the first step in destroying something fragile, and she might as well finish it for him.

But by the middle of the afternoon four light golden loaves stood cooling on the bench, and Nerida was proud of them. She stood back and admired them openly. After all, there was no one to see this and comment.

Sandy and Margaret were both dozing on the verandah, and Leigh had taken all four children upstream to the rock cliffs on an 'afternoon tea picnic', saying to Nerida, 'You've got to keep an eye on your bread, and

Margaret and Sandy shouldn't be left alone. Besides, I'm sure you'd like a little break from the kids' company.'

For a moment Nerida bristled at the way he had arranged her afternoon, and thought of saying that no, actually she'd much prefer to come on the picnic, but it wasn't the truth, and he was right about Margaret and Sandy anyway.

'Don't forget the blanket trick if any more planes come over,' was his parting remark as the little group set off, with Joe grinning from his position in the old pram, and Sam crowing with excitement as he was perched on the doctor's shoulders. Lucy and Ross were already scampering ahead.

'Have a good time, then,' Nerida called rather thinly after him, but he did not turn and he did not reply, and while they had been talking he had not met her gaze.

She settled herself on the verandah with the others and began to read, Leigh having found what seemed like a goldmine in the shed this morning—a small crate of very old and dusty hardback novels. They had only thought to bring books for the children from the new homestead.

It was the first real relaxation and escape she had had since . . . when? What was today? Saturday. And she had made that fateful visit to Reid's Nursing Agency on Wednesday morning. Did Sydney still exist? She felt that it might have slid off into the sea for all the reality it had for her now. And as for London . . . !

It was impossible to concentrate on reading, and even the coffee at her side grew cold before it was half drunk. She found that she was constantly listening—for the children's laughter echoing in the rocks upsteam, or a playful shout from Leigh; for the sound of another plane; or for the sound of that flood-crest which they knew must come soon, and which added, always, an undercurrent of tension that was rarely spoken of.

Would they ever get out of here at all? Perhaps they'd been completely forgotten, and would go on living here for ever like latter-day Robinson Crusoes. Sandy would fade away into death eventually, the children would grow up, and she and Leigh would . . .

No, stop! Those thoughts bordered on craziness. Was that what would happen to them all if they weren't got out of here soon?

They *would* get out of here soon! An entire load of passengers and an RFDS Nomad couldn't disappear without a search being mounted, and a major one at that. Even though they would have started off looking in the wrong area, they'd get here eventually.

Firmly she took a gulp of cold coffee, picked up her book, and began to read.

CHAPTER NINE

'WE WAS going to wait for the travelling pastor feller to come up through our way. Bridie made a dress, beautiful it was. She wanted to be properly married, and so did I. Some fellers didn't wait. Some fellers did things they shouldn't have. Poor lubras* didn't know any better, lost their old ways. My Bridget wanted to wait for the travelling pastor feller, but he didn't come, and he didn't come. And then the rains, they *did* come . . .' Sandy trailed off for a moment, lost in his story.

It was completely silent in the lounge-room of the old homestead. Only the fire glowing in the hearth hissed and crackled a little. Nerida didn't dare to move in case the old man got distracted. Out of the corner of her eye she saw that Leigh and Margaret were frozen too, almost holding their breath.

The children were safely in bed and it was getting late. Sandy had sung again after the evening meal, and had recited some poems, old Australian classics by Henry Lawson and 'Banjo' Patterson, that he must have learnt years ago during his few years of schooling, or had heard repeated around a campfire.

Then he had started to talk about his life, just snippets of rambling anecdote at first, but prompted gently by Margaret and Leigh, his stories had become clearer, his memories more vivid, and finally, a little while ago, he had begun to talk of Bridie.

Some gasses trapped in the burning wood popped suddenly, and released a shower of hissing golden sparks. Sandy spoke again.

'I couldn't stay at Dargo much longer—had to be at Windorah to drive a big mob through up north. Decided

* Aboriginal women

151

we'd ride up to Windorah together. She was a treat on a horse, my Bridget. We set out, we had one good day, we made a good distance. Rained in the night, all night. Creeks came up and we couldn't get through, not forward, not back.' He stopped again and took some tea, his thin old mouth in the rim of the cup for a long time. 'Then Bridie got crook. Didn't know what to do. She was burning all over—fever. Two days she didn't know me. She couldn't eat, and I couldn't either. I was too worried about her. Three days, four days. The creeks were down again, but she was too sick to travel. I just built a little shelter for her out of branches, and hoped someone'd come along. It was all I could do. But no one came. The horses were real worried; they were like that, good horses, they could tell. Then one morning—forget how many days by this time—she'd been having a little sleep. I was real pleased because she hadn't slept much, she was too fevered. She woke up and she opened her eyes, she knew me and my heart jumped up in my chest, and I thought, she's going to live, she's going to be all right. And then she said my name. I was holding her. "Alex," she said. Alex, she called me, not Sandy. Some people called me Alex back in them days—long time ago. "Alex." And then I got worried—her eyes was too bright. I kept holding her, waiting till she'd say something more. And she just died. She died just there like that. Two hours later an old Ford truck came through with that travelling pastor. We buried Bridie and I went on up to Windorah.'

Nerida wiped her face fiercely with the back of her hand and held her aching throat tight. She could have sobbed at the story, but somehow she knew it would upset the old man. It was like nursing in a hospital sometimes if a patient was dying. It could be crueller to give way to your own emotion than to remain calm. Neither Leigh nor Margaret spoke, and she could not risk looking at them.

'I went on up to Windorah,' Sandy repeated quietly. He was not asking for a response. Perhaps he had even

forgotten who his audience was. And any words would
have been trite and dreadful.

The silence continued for minutes and then, almost
imperceptibly, it began to be broken. At first Nerida
thought it was just wind in the chimney and round the
corners of the house, then she wondered confusedly
about thunder, although she knew the night was still
clear. She turned questioningly to Leigh and saw that he
was listening too.

'The flood-crest,' he said softly. 'That's the roar of it in
the gorge upstream. We'd hear it much louder if we were
still at the new homestead.'

'Thank God we're not!' Margaret exclaimed
fervently.

'What . . . will it be like?' asked Nerida hesitantly.
'What will it look like?'

'Come and see,' said Leigh, stretching out his hand to
help her up from where she lay curled on a blanket by the
fire.

She took it without thinking, forgetting that they were
to be 'professional' in their distance from one another
from now on. But he dropped his arm abruptly as soon as
she was safely on her feet, and she guessed that he had
suddenly become aware of what he had done and wanted
to step back from it.

'Margaret, would you like to see it too?' he asked. 'I
could carry you out.'

'I'll look from the window. It's all right.'

She was lying on Leigh's bed, and needed only to roll
over carefully in order to see outside.

Sandy stood up shakily, alarm creasing his old
features into a shape completely different from the one
they had fallen into as he told the story of Bridie. He had
registered that something was happening in the present,
and it had been a shock for him to have to relinquish
the softer, hazier world of the past, filled though it
was with memories that must once have been very
painful.

'Sit down, Sandy, it's all right,' Leigh said calmly.

'What's happening? What's happening?' The roar was getting louder now.

Leigh tried to coax him with gentle arms back into his seat by the fire, but the old man was too agitated, and only gripped Leigh's arm, shaking it insistently.

'It's the flood-crest,' Leigh explained.

But Sandy seemed not to understand. The effort of singing and speaking and telling his story had tired out his old mind and he could not grasp anything.

'This isn't Coolamon. Where's this? What's happening?' he demanded.

'No, this is Jerilda, remember? Good old Jerilda!' Leigh used the old man's own words, but it didn't seem to help.

'Good old Jerilda,' Sandy repeated blankly. He was distracted for a moment, puzzled, then agitated again. 'What's happening? Why am I here? Where's my home?'

'It's all right, Sandy old love,' Margaret said soothingly. 'You're here with the Kellys now, remember? You live with the Kellys now.'

'Where's Ron? Where's Ron Kelly?'

'Ron's out with the stock.'

'Is he?'

'Yes, he and Jack and Herbert are looking after the stock. They're taking them over to Lacey's Bore.'

But Sandy only sat down in his chair again and began wringing his trembling hands and mumbling incoherently in an agitation that meant he was almost moaning.

'You two go out and have a look,' said Margaret. 'I'll keep an eye on him.'

'Coming, Nerida?'

'Yes.'

'Bring a blanket. It's cold out there.'

They stood in silence on the verandah, listening and watching. The wide band of water seemed still like a lake, and was bright with the reflection of the moonlight. Nothing could be seen as yet, but the sound grew louder, and birds of all kinds could be heard squawking and calling in fear at the incomprehensible disturbance.

It was eerie to be standing here with Leigh, like spectators at a parade, waiting for something to appear, thrill, and pass on. Nerida was still unsure about what to expect. It was cold and still—it seemed that any wind during the day almost always dropped at sunset—and there was little to say.

The water, when it came, was like an unending ocean wave, continually foaming and breaking, but dirty with silt and sand, and filled with debris gathered on its journey. Nerida shuddered when she thought of how it would have been at the new homestead when that tumbling slope of water, at least six feet high, came crashing through.

Up here, quite safe, it was easy to underestimate the power and force of its sheer volume, but it needed only a little imagination to put yourself in front of that wave and experience some of the fear that would come as it moved unstoppably towards you. If it had come yesterday while they were in the boat . . . They might have been just another part of the matchstick debris tossed on the crest of the wave.

'It's gone. It's subsiding,' Leigh said later.

Nerida did not know how much time had passed since they had first seen it. Half an hour? She was stiff and cold, but the fascination of the sight was only just starting to pall.

'But it won't be back to today's level until tomorrow night at the earliest, I would think,' Leigh added.

'And then?'

'And then it'll all just gradually dry out and drain away over the next weeks,' he said. 'The country's used to it. It'll be lush and green for a while—millions of flowers. The cattle, the ones that have survived—which we hope will be most of them—will be fat for a season, then, no doubt, we'll have a drought. That's the way it works out here. Never a happy medium.'

Nerida was silent. It was all so far outside of her range

of experience, and her imagination could not encompass it all either.

'But of course you'll be long gone by then,' were Leigh's next dismissive words. 'Coming back in?'

'Oh . . . Yes, of course,' she said distantly, covering a strange new pain with the words.

Leigh's comment had been a reminder, and deliberate, she was sure, of how temporary and unimportant a fixture she was here. It was a fact that became harder to reconcile all the time. How could this world, and Leigh, disappear from her life as if they had never been, when the intensity of this experience was something she had never known before? When rescue came, as it must eventually, surely there would be something she could hang on to and take with her into the rest of her life, something apart from a memory that would fade inexorably, a lesson or two learnt about herself.

'It's no good,' she realised. 'I simply can't think about life after this at all. This is all that's real for me at the moment. It's all I want to be real.'

And a good part of the reason for that was Leigh. When she had shut the night air out of the warm room again, she saw that he was crouched in front of the fire, his thighs hard beneath his blue jeans. He was holding his raw red palms out to the flames, and was dabbing some vitamin A ointment on to the sorest patches.

There had been another splinter in his left hand tonight after his work with the axe this morning, but he hadn't asked Nerida to help him get it out. She had come across him poking at it with the tweezers in the kitchen after the evening meal, and had had to clench her teeth to prevent the escape of a cry of disappointment. She had laid the dirty dishes she was carring abruptly on the sink and had left the room again immediately, pretending she had not even noticed what he was doing.

He looked up, now, as she went over to warm her own extremities, put the ointment aside quickly, and turned his palms down as if he too was aware of the change between them tonight. Well, it had been at his instigation!

'We should have thought to wake the children up to watch,' Margaret said sleepily. 'It was quite a sight.'

'Yes, we weren't thinking,' nodded Leigh. 'Perhaps we'd better not tell them how fascinating it was. But where's Sandy?'

The old man had not been in the room when they returned, and Margaret was suddenly alert again.

'Oh, heavens! I must have dropped off to sleep without realising it. He got quite calm again and was sitting in that chair. He's so restless, though. I might have known he wouldn't stay there.'

'He's probably in his room,' said Leigh. 'I'll carry you off to bed and then have a look.'

'Need me to help?' asked Nerida.

'No, it's all right. Go to bed yourself if you like. It's late.'

He scooped up Margaret's bulky form with surprising ease, and Nerida didn't stir. She was enjoying the feeling of being alone by the fire. She could hear sounds from the bathroom and bedroom as Leigh helped Margaret, and it was just enough to keep her awake, which was good, as she didn't want to repeat last night's scenario of falling asleep here, with its unsettling consequences.

Then the back door opened and Sandy came in with his usual shuffle. He had been wandering outside for some reason, and was agitated again. Nerida went to him and tried to get him to settle, without success.

'Perhaps he needs a tranquilliser or something to make him sleep,' she said anxiously to Leigh when he returned, but he only shook his head curtly.

'I'd rather not unless we have to. Once you start that kind of thing, it's difficult to stop. He's been so healthy all his life . . . and Margaret couldn't cope with him at Coolamon Creek if he was zonked out on pills. Often it has to be done, of course, but with Sandy I'm hoping not. I'm hoping he'll slip gently away one day before he needs to be sent to a home or kept permanently on medication. I suppose it's pigheaded of me,' he grinned suddenly.

'It's not,' Nerida said, absurdly joyful about the fact that they were communicating again. 'I see what you mean. But perhaps you can do more to settle him than I can.'

'What you really mean is that it *is* pigheaded and I have to take the consequences,' replied Leigh.

'You said it,' said Nerida, daring to be flip.

'Get to bed, Nurse!'

The following day was strangely uneventful. Life here in this unreal situation seemed already to have fallen into a pattern and routine. They had been waiting for two events, and one of them had passed. The children were disappointed to have missed the sight, of course, but forgot it quickly.

'It's not fair! I thought I heard something in the night,' was all Lucy said. 'But I thought it was just in my dream. I wish I'd woken up properly.'

'Yes, I heard it in my dream, too,' nodded Ross in earnest agreement, trying hard as usual to keep up with his livewire of a big sister.

Now there was just one thing to wait for, and waiting was all they could do, it seemed, although once Nerida caught Leigh gazing thoughtfully at the dinghy he had dragged up out of reach of the waters. She felt an absurd fear clutch at her heart. He wasn't thinking of setting off somewhere in that tub, was he?

She wanted to ask him about it, to obtain reassurance, but didn't dare. He had scarcely spoken to her today, and it was clearly deliberate, although no one else had noticed anything. In fact, rather the contrary.

'Why aren't you married?' Lucy had asked Nerida bluntly as they washed up the breakfast dishes together. Mercifully, Leigh wasn't around to hear the question. Somehow it was a subject she would have hated to discuss in his hearing.

'No reason,' she had replied lightly to Lucy's probe.

But the little girl was insistent as ever. 'There must be a reason.'

'Maybe I don't want to be.'

'Yes, you do,' Lucy said definitely.

'Well then, I just haven't met the right person.'

'What about Leigh?'

Nerida almost choked, but said steadily, 'I've only known Leigh for four days.'

'Oh, have you? Oh, well, I suppose it's too soon to say.' Lucy was clearly disappointed. 'But it could be a good idea, couldn't it?'

'I don't think so, Lucy,' said Nerida carefully. She didn't want to protest too much, either. 'Thank you for the suggestion, though.'

'That's OK,' Lucy shrugged.

'Um . . . you won't say anything like that to Leigh, will you?' said Nerida warily.

'Why not?'

Nerida hunted desperately for a good reason. 'Well, it's not the sort of thing you say to men.'

'Isn't it?'

'No.'

'OK then.' Lucy had shrugged again as she wiped the last plate, then suddenly dashed madly out the back door calling, 'There's a snake! I saw a snake!'

Fortunately, but to Lucy's disappointment, it turned out to be only a large goanna lizard, but Nerida had blessed the creature anyway, for saving her from a very uncomfortable topic of conversation, and one that had a strange sting in it.

She had only known Leigh for four days, and he certainly didn't seem to want to get to know her any better. In a few days more at the most, she would be gone from this place, and probably a few days after that she would be gone from his life for ever. Already she felt the loss as a deep hurt, and wondered rather bemusedly how it had all happened.

'I was a girl who got engaged to a boy I'd known for a hundred years,' she thought. 'Who am I now?'

Margaret had not had a twinge of pain since Friday afternoon, and it was now Sunday, but she remained patient and cheerful about lying down, as Leigh felt it was not yet safe for her to move about. Sandy had calmed down after his story-telling and restless agitation of the night before, and was quiet during the day, eating well and poking vaguely around the two outbuildings when he was not seated on the verandah gazing out over the flooded landscape.

Leigh was very satisfied with Sam's condition too, and Joe had said in his usual shy way, 'Foot not hurtin' hardly at all now.' Lucy and Ross, of course, had never been a cause for concern, and so there was little for Nerida and Leigh to do in their capacity as medical people, apart from keeping on with Margaret's steroid injections, which Leigh had decided to do.

That did not mean they were idle, though. Meals to prepare, the kitchen stove to keep stoked, children to entertain—this time with an expedition downstream in search of interesting plant or animal life and to look at some of the debris left behind by the flood. And the ever-present undercurrent of listening for a plane or a helicopter that still did not come.

'Are we going to live here for ever?' little Ross asked that night as they sat in front of the fire. They were spending another quiet evening—what else could they do?—after the meal of tinned Irish stew, salad, and potatoes done in their jackets in the coals, that Nerida had prepared with the children's offered 'help'.

'No, love,' Margaret replied.

'But we've been here for a long time.' It only seemed that way to Ross, with his child's way of measuring time and experience—but Nerida realised that it was starting to seem that way to her too.

'Well, what's happening, then?' Ross persisted when no one replied to his last statement. There was the hint of a grizzle in his tone. 'When are we going to see Dad?'

'Soon, love,' Margaret replied, wearily this time. She

must be worried about Ron, although with an outback-bred stoicism, she never said so.

'But when's soon?'

'We don't know, silly,' Lucy put in. 'When we're rescued.'

'Well, I want to be rescued tomorrow.'

He fell asleep soon after that, as it was past his normal bedtime and he had walked quite a bit during the day. Leigh carried him off to bed as he had done the first night they had spent here, but the child's words continued to drum in Nerida's mind.

For the children, the novelty was wearing off. It would be harder to entertain them and keep them happy tomorrow; they would be more restless and more irritable. This was not a holiday, with entertainments and new things to see and do, nor was it like normal life, where there was a routine for them of School of the Air, beloved pets, tasks around the homestead, bush skills like horse-riding to acquire.

Something had to happen soon. 'Tomorrow', as Ross had said. Nerida felt this very strongly, and somehow, in spite of their distance from each other today, she knew that Leigh felt it too.

'I'm just about ready to hit the hay as well, Leigh, when you've dealt with Lucy and Joe and Sam,' Margaret confessed, yawning hugely, when he returned from tucking in little Ross. 'It sounds dreadful when all I've been doing is lying around. But pregnancy makes you tired, and really, it's not relaxing for any of us here, wondering when something's going to happen. Although you two are performing miracles getting us so organised and safe.'

It was the first time that Nerida had heard a note of complaint from Margaret, and it seemed ominous. Instinctively she flicked her gaze towards Leigh, and saw his fists clench suddenly and his brow darken into a set of deep furrows, but he replied steadily and easily.

'Yes, it isn't easy. Of course I'll take you to bed.'

'And I'll do Sam and Lucy,' Nerida put in, glad to

have a task to perform to dispel the edge of fear that had
crept up on her.

'What about you, Sandy?' Leigh asked cheerfully.

'Oh yes, bedtime for old Sandy,' the old man agreed,
his eyes clearing for a moment, then dulling again.
'Bedtime for me. Long day on the track tomorrow. Lot
of cattle.'

'You go along then, and you can sing some songs for
Joe. Help him get to sleep too.'

Joe grinned, his teeth very white in the firelight in his
dark, frank-featured face. 'Yes, song'd be good, wou'n't
it, old Sandy. I'll sing you a song too.'

Which left just Leigh and Nerida by the fire twenty
minutes later when everyone else was settled. It should
have been easy simply to yawn and stretch, say she was
tired and go, but Leigh had made coffee and held a
steaming mug out to her, and she felt she couldn't have
refused even if she had wanted to—which, weakly, she
didn't.

It was the first friendly gesture he had made to her
today.

They sat and sipped in silence for a while. Nerida
couldn't help watching the play of golden light from the
lamp and the fire on his tanned face and in his dark hair.
It brought out coppery glints there that she had not
consciously noticed before. He was staring into the
flames, frowning darkly again, and she longed to ask him
if it was Ross's innocent complaint and Margaret's unusual note of impatience that was worrying him. She
didn't dare to, though, too afraid that it would only
break this rather peaceful mood between them.

And so it was Leigh who spoke first.

'I feel a bit like a naughty schoolboy for suggesting
this,' he said, deadpan. 'But . . . I slipped in the rest of
that port in one of our loads. Thought it might have been
useful for Sandy—old people need their habits—but
Margaret tells me he took the pledge in 1924, so if it's not
to go to waste . . .'

'Won't it keep?' Nerida asked innocently, thrilling to

the fact that they actually seemed to be talking like normal human beings, but not wanting to let it show.

He just grinned and poured half an inch into two mugs. 'Excuse the state of the glassware.'

He was sprawled lazily on the floor, the neck of his denim shirt open, and Nerida suddenly felt silly and missish perched tightly in the shabby old armchair that Sandy had vacated. She got up to put a log on the fire, as a prelude to changing her position, but then her courage failed her and she returned to the chair.

'I wanted him to kiss me,' she realised. 'And I thought if I lay on the blanket closer to him, it would happen. What a fool I am!'

They talked for a long while about a great many things. Nerida felt she could have stayed there all night just for the pleasure of listening to the low, resonant timbre of Leigh's voice and the occasional chuckle of intelligent laughter, and of gazing at the flickering shadows that played over his firm body in the firelight.

There was immense pleasure, too, in sharing opinions, in finding that she had much in common with him and much to respect about him. Most of all, it was so good to sense that the tension and hostility within him had drained away for whatever reason, leaving him warm and open.

Finally, though, Nerida knew that she had to make a move towards her own bed. It was so hard to wilfully break this mood, but she made herself stretch slowly and lazily out of her chair and say, 'I'm tired. I should have gone to bed long ago.'

Leigh looked up suddenly at her movement, as if startled, and his eyes darkened, but he said nothing. She waited, standing by the fire to warm her hands, unable to say a final good night just yet. Leigh stood up and crossed the small space that separated them.

'Good night then, Nerida.' He took hold of her shoulders very lightly with his raw hands and bent towards her. 'I'll say this now, in case there isn't the chance again: I couldn't have got through all this without you.'

'Without me? But I've done so little! A bit of rowing to save your hands . . .' She had to force herself to meet the blue eyes that were looking steadily in her own dark ones. 'I've felt so helpless and . . .'

She didn't finish, because gently he had drowned the words with his lips, murmuring her name softly between kisses that were at first brief and tantalising and teasing, then long, slow and insistent. Each one sent fire coursing through her veins, and she responded instinctively and completely without stopping to question anything at all.

Their kiss seemed timeless here in the desert in the silent house with everyone else asleep behind closed doors. It did not matter if it went on for ever. His arms were around her, caressing the soft curves of her slim figure, and her own hands explored the firm shape of his back. His lips travelled down to her neck, and to her ear, her forehead, her eyes. She nuzzled her face into the curve above his collarbone, tingling all over at the warm sweet male scent that hovered there.

The kerosene lamp flickered wildly for a minute and then died, plunging the room into an orange dimness that owed its only light to the dying coals of the fire.

It might have been this that meant there was no turning back, or it might simply have been themselves and their own need. Whatever it was, when Nerida felt Leigh pull away a little and brush his fingers lightly down her throat and then begin to slip undone the pearly buttons that fastened her pale grey blouse, to find and cup her firm breasts, she did nothing to stop him.

Moments later, the dim light glowed richly on bodies that were unfettered and unseparated by clothing, and it seemed that the only possible and natural and right thing to do was to sink to the floor in a tangle of limbs and hair and caresses, and continue the journey of discovery of each other.

'Nerida!' her name was a caress on his lips, which were exploring every inch of her now, arousing her skin, her breasts, and the secret places of her body into urgent and tingling awareness. Her hands kneaded his muscular

flesh and pressed him closer to her as they guided each
other wordlessly to the right places.

There was just one pause before they were both
committed to ultimate fulfilment, and although it
momentarily bruised the mood it was a part of Leigh
that Nerida had to respect—his sense of shared responsibility.

'Is it safe?' he flung out in a low groan.

'Yes, yes, about as safe as it could be. I'm pretty
regular . . .'

'That's all I wanted to know, my darling.'

And then they were tangled together again in a
mounting crescendo of unified eagerness and delight
that spent itself finally and left them breathless and still
entwined. The fire hissed and a brief gust of wind sang in
the chimney, but aside from that it was very quiet.
Nerida wanted to speak, to let words of love and joy
come tumbling forth and to hear Leigh's answering
commitment in return, but she was too afraid that any
words, even the most right ones, would break this spell
of perfect unity between them.

Leigh stretched an arm back, pulled a blanket from his
bed and tucked it around them, then they simply lay
there with Nerida's head cradled on his chest so she
could hear the beat of his heart and feel the rise and fall
of his breathing, while he laced his fingers through her
hair and caressed its silky waves. It was so perfect to lie
here like this that she hoped the night might never end.

CHAPTER TEN

It was cold, and Nerida's hip felt bruised by the hard surface beneath her. Her limbs were stiff and her hair was tangled across her face and in her mouth. There was no pillow, nothing to cushion her head . . .

She woke up with a start. This wasn't her bed at all, that was why. This was the floor in front of the hearth in the lounge-room of the old homestead. Her eyes snapped open and with a cold shock she was suddenly able to take in every detail of her situation. The fire had died into grey ashes, the blanket was twisted scratchily and inadequately around her still-naked body, and Leigh was gone.

Had he simply moved to the narrow bed he usually occupied, that was only a few feet away? She twisted abruptly and sat up to look, cricking her neck painfully as she did so, and having to rake away a tangle of limp hair before she could see. The bed was flat and hard, and there was no one in the room but herself.

Going stiffly to the window, awkward in the blanket, she could see the first grey wash of dawn light low on the eastern horizon, and she shivered. It was the coldest hour of the night. How long had she been alone? When had Leigh left, and where had he gone?

Perhaps he had gone to sleep in her own room next to Sam's little bed. She wanted desperately to see him. The magic of last night seemed to have died with the fire, she felt sore all over, and needed urgently for him to take her in his arms again and tell her that what they had done last night had been right and important, and had meant the same to him as it had to her.

Unable to wait, needing to see him now, Nerida turned from the window and stepped across the space in front of the hearth towards the door. Something soft caught at her feet and almost tripped her over. She had to reach out and grab the arm of Sandy's tatty old chair to steady herself. She stepped aside and looked down.

It was her own discarded clothing that had caught her, the garments still flung carelessly where Leigh had dropped them as he had caressingly undressed her. She picked them up hastily and bundled them together, then went quickly out of the room. Leigh's clothes had not been there. He must be in her own bed, although goodness knew why he had gone there.

She opened the door and peered into the darkness. Sam breathed rhythmically and made some little wet noises. He was sucking his thumb. But her own bed was empty and unslept in. She should get into it herself, and try to snatch an hour's further rest before the day began, but she had never felt less like sleep. Where was Leigh?

Moving quietly and carefully so as not to wake Sam, Nerida gathered clean underwear, tights and her nurse's uniform and cardigan. A uniform and cardigan weren't very practical for this place, but she had washed them the day before yesterday, and her other clothes were beginning to feel very stale.

Her hair felt limp, too, after Leigh's caresses. She had shampoo and conditioner in her sponge-bag in the bathroom, and hoped they would be enough to counteract the salty, stiffening effect of the bore-water.

She showered in the dark, hoping the sound of the water would not wake anyone, then dried herself on one of the towels they had brought from the Winthrops', and dressed. If Leigh had still not appeared, she would go for a walk. It would be cold at first in these clothes, but she would walk fast, and the sun would soon appear. It was going to be another clear, cloudless day.

Leigh hadn't appeared, and she no longer wanted to openly look for him. A cold hand of fear was beginning to squeeze at her heart. She felt abandoned by him, and that it must be deliberate. Last night's glowing golden mood had completely gone, and she no longer believed in the utter unity she had felt with him then. Perhaps he had been driven simply by male need, not by real care at all. She knew that that happened all too often.

'Not Leigh!' her heart insisted. 'Leigh's not like that!'

But how could she know, really? And with the evidence of this morning—his cold absence from the room when she woke—her fear started to seem very real.

She walked upstream from the homestead, telling herself that it would be good to explore the broken, rocky cliffs a little further. Although she had come part of the way with the children yesterday afternoon, they had taken too much of her attention, and she had not absorbed much of the landscape.

The air was crisp and invigorating, and dawn colour was beginning to brighten the trees, the smoothly slipping water and the red ground. It would have been a beautiful and exhilarating walk if she had been able to enjoy it. She found a perch on a smooth knob of rock and decided just to sit there and watch. It would be cold, but she could put up with that, and she would see more if she was still.

The birds were beginning to chatter in the trees, the water below rippled as frogs plopped in and out, and then she saw the grey shapes of kangaroos going down to the water's edge back below the homestead. Some of them were approaching from her direction, and passed quite close by, since she sat so still, without seeing her. Their strong legs thudded on the ground and the momentum of the swing of their powerful tails carried them forward, then they slowed and lolloped along using the delicate front paws as well as their hind legs.

It was several minutes before Nerida picked out another figure down below the homestead near the water's edge. It was Leigh, and he had disturbed the animals, though Nerida could see he was aware of them and was trying not to. What on earth was he doing?

Then she realised. He was dragging the old dinghy back down towards the water and loading it with supplies. He couldn't be planning to return them all to the new homestead. Nerida knew that the place would not be fit for human habitation at the moment, if it had survived the onslaught of the flood-crest at all. So . . . ?

There was only one answer. He was planning to set off downstream in search of help somewhere. For one mad moment she wanted to scramble to her feet and run back to him, fling herself on him and tell him not to go, but with a tremendous effort of will she stifled the impulse. It would be a disastrous action.

The sun had risen now, and its first thin rays stretched across the red earth and struck her back, giving faint warmth and casting her shadow in a long slant to the left. Leigh went back up the slope and disappeared inside the house. He had not seen her. He had not looked. Probably he assumed she was in her own bed.

Should she go back? There were plenty of things to do. She could get the kitchen fire going, put on the kettle for coffee or tea, begin making toast and frying eggs and cooking tinned frankfurters and tomatoes, as well as preparing cereal and dried fruit for Margaret and anyone else who wanted it. The others would be awake soon. Sam would need dressing, and Margaret should have help as she washed. Joe's foot dressing was ready to be changed again too.

But instead she sat on, relishing the oasis of aloneness, dreading what she would see in Leigh's face when she returned—rejection and coldness, or, perhaps even worse, simply indifference.

There came a time, though, when she could no longer ignore the fact that the sun was well above the horizon and full of real warmth. She had to go back.

Leigh was in the kitchen when she reached the old homestead, and the crisp sizzle and savoury aroma of the breakfast she herself had planned hit her senses immediately.

'Shall I take Mum hers in bed?' came Lucy's voice.

'I'll take her tea,' Ross put in.

So both the Kelly children were in the kitchen with Leigh. Probably the others were up and dressed now as well. Would Leigh be angry about her absence?

He looked up as she entered the warm kitchen and his expression was instantly guarded and unreadable.

'Hullo, Neddie. You're wearing your uniform,' said Lucy.

'Does that mean we're going home today?' Ross asked.

'No, I suppose she was just sick of her other clothes. I'm sick of mine too,' Lucy replied. 'And you've been for a walk, haven't you?'

'Yes, it was lovely. I saw kangaroos coming down to drink, and all sorts of things,' Nerida told them.

'Ross and me are taking breakfast in for Mummy.'

'I might come with you, then, and say hullo,' Nerida replied hastily. She would avoid being alone with Leigh if she possibly could.

Margaret stretched and smiled when she saw Nerida and the children.

'How are you today?' asked Nerida.

'Sick of lying down,' Margaret replied.

'Well, I know this won't help, but some pregnant women—if they're having a multiple birth, or if they have a low-lying placenta, for example—have to spend two or three months lying in hospital,' Nerida told her.

'Oh, lordy-loo!' Margaret exclaimed with feeling. 'I'd go crackers!'

Sam's little feet came pattering down the passage and he flung himself on 'Neddie', who was sitting on the end of the bed, for a cuddle. Margaret began her breakfast, with the children chattering brightly to entertain her.

Then Leigh appeared in the doorway. Nerida looked up instinctively, their eyes met for a moment, then hastily skated away from each other. Nerida knew that she had stiffened and flushed hotly, and she buried her face in Sam's hair and gave him a loud kiss in an attempt to disguise her turbulent feelings. She felt a hundred miles away from Leigh, and it wasn't by *her* inclination.

'Out of the room for a sec, kids,' Leigh said cheerfully.

'You're going to discuss important things,' Lucy accused immediately. 'Why can't we stay?'

'Because Joe is lonely. He's having his breakfast on the verandah all by himself.'

'What about Sandy?'

'Sandy's not much company for a boy, most of the time, is he?'

'OK, we'll go,' grumbled Lucy, hauling Ross to his feet. 'Come on, brother.'

'OK, sister.'

'I've made a decision,' said Leigh as soon as they had left and shut the door. 'I'm going to take the dinghy and go downstream to Billabong Creek. I can't just go on waiting here like this.'

Nerida said nothing. She had known it already, but she noticed that he had said 'I can't go on waiting', not 'We'. It was an unconscious slip, but she knew he had been thinking of his own discomfort about waiting cooped up with her, after what had happened last night.

'He wants to avoid me,' she thought. 'It was a one-night stand for him, and now he wants to forget all about me. He doesn't want to get involved, so he's going to escape.'

'But, Leigh, that's eighty miles!' Margaret exclaimed after a stunned pause. 'More than that if you think of the way the creek meanders. It'll take days!'

'Two days, perhaps,' said Leigh. 'I hope much less. Maybe more if I'm unlucky. It depends on the current and on the state of the channel, and on how much I can row with my hands.'

He held out his raw palms for a moment and then closed his fists carefully, hiding them, but not before Nerida had seen the pain the action caused.

'You can't go like that!' she burst out, regretting the words almost before they were spoken. Or rather, regretting the tone. It had not been the clinical assessment of a nurse, but the passionate reaction of a woman who did not want to see the man she loved in pain.

'I'll bandage them before I go,' he shrugged.

'That won't be good enough.'

'Let me make that judgement, Nerida.' His tone was

hard. 'I've packed the boat with everything I'll need, and I've had breakfast—I was up before dawn. I'm going to leave straight away.'

'No!' The passionate syllable died in Nerida's throat. It was a naked betrayal of her need, but she found a way to deny it, saying immediately, 'I'm sorry—I'm wrong. Please ignore that. I was just . . . frightened, that's all, about being left to cope here without you, but after all, everything's fine now, really.'

Leigh did not speak and neither did Margaret, then he opened the door to go.

'I'll do my hands and then say goodbye to the children. They'll think it's an adventure.'

'Leigh . . .' It was Margaret, holding out her arms to him in a gesture that Nerida would have given so much to be able to make.

'No goodbyes, Margaret,' he said, not moving from the door. 'We'll be seeing each other again very soon, in Benanda.'

Then he had disappeared. Nerida wanted to go after him, to at least wave him off downstream in the old dinghy, and watch him until he disappeared, but she knew that his 'No goodbyes' had really been meant for her. He had not even wanted to touch her in a friendly gesture of farewell. She felt utterly desolate, and last night seemed like a distant golden dream that was beginning, with hindsight, to take on the qualities of a nightmare.

Margaret had resumed her breakfast, clearly worried about Leigh, but taking it with her usual outback stoicism. In a minute she would probably begin to chat, and Nerida knew that she could not bear it.

'I'll go and put on the kettle for more tea,' she said, craving aloneness.

'Right, love.'

She filled the kettle full and then hid in the kitchen till it boiled, first hearing Leigh's hard footsteps as he left the house after bandaging his hands, then the scamper of the children as they ran down to see him off. She made the tea slowly and carefully, taking a strange brief comfort in the mesmerising flow of the amber liquid from the spout, and the curls of steam rising from the cups.

He would be gone now, and perhaps already out of sight. If she could save herself from betraying her feelings to the others, it was safe to leave the kitchen.

The long morning passed very slowly. Nerida helped Margaret to wash and dress, then supported her so that she could walk out to the verandah and lie there on a mattress with pillows and blankets. Lucy and Ross helped Sandy to split more kindling, more for something to do than because it was really needed.

Nerida washed the dishes and tidied the kitchen, then invented some new games for Joe and Sam to play in the back yard, which Lucy and Ross joined in on after they'd had enough of the kindling. She made more tea for Sandy and Margaret, who were both inveterate drinkers of the stuff, then she sat with them on the verandah with a cup of coffee for herself.

Leigh's words of four days ago, said very seriously as they stood by the outbuilding of the new homestead, kept drumming in her head. 'If something should happen to me . . .' What if something did happen? The possibility was now, starkly, real.

It was impossible not to stare downstream in the direction he had gone, as if he might magically appear from there again, although that was ridiculous. And it would only cause her heartache to see him anyway. She was bitterly regretting last night. What had she done but wilfully open a channel of feeling within her which she should have known could lead only in one direction—to pain!

Involuntarily, she let out a heavy sigh. Margaret heard it and turned her head sympathetically.

'It's getting harder, isn't it?' she said. 'At first there was so much to do, we had no time to think about anything beyond the moment and getting to safety ourselves. And I had the baby to worry about. Now it's different. We've got time on our hands. I just keep thinking and worrying about Ron.' Her voice choked briefly as she said her husband's name. 'Hoping he's all right, hoping he's not sitting somewhere worrying about me and the kids. It must be like that for you. Somewhere there's someone you're worrying about and thinking about, who's worrying and thinking about you.'

'Yes,' Nerida nodded, although it wasn't really true. Leigh was in her mind constantly, but she would not be in his.

As for the 'outside world' . . . Parents, sister and friends seemed so far away. Would they even have heard that she was missing? Actually, yes, by now perhaps they would, and if they had, they would be terribly worried. She felt a sudden pang of love and concern for them, and it came almost as a relief. She *did* have bonds somewhere, even though her bond with Leigh was irrevocably broken.

What had he said last night? 'I'll say this now, in case there isn't the chance again.' If she had really thought at the time about what those words meant she would have known that he had no intention of seeing her again after all this was over. She burned again at the memory of what had followed—burned with regret, but also, inescapably, with longing and love.

Margaret was speaking again. 'It must be very hard for Leigh too, worrying about Jenny. I suppose that's why he decided to go off to Billabong Creek. Just couldn't stand having nothing to do. He's very active—for a doctor,' she amended.

It was an unconscious comparison with her own bush-bred husband, probably, and it might have amused Nerida if this had been yesterday, but it wasn't yesterday, and what had those words about 'Jenny' meant? She had to know.

'Worrying about Jenny?' she heard herself repeat questioningly, in a high, thin voice.

'Yes, the poor girl, Sister Walters, whose father died so suddenly. Oh, of course, that was why you had to

come up, so you'd know who I mean. Well, she and
Leigh had been going out together before it all happened. It must have been a wrench, with Jenny's plans so
uncertain. I'm sure Leigh must be desperate to find out
what's going on.'

'Yes, he must be.' The words were an incredible
effort, spoken through a throat that was tight as a vice.

Surely this was too cruel! That Leigh had been in love
with Jenny all along . . . Nerida felt cheap and humiliated and angry and terribly, terribly hurt, but somehow,
somehow, she *must not* let it show, *must not* let Margaret
guess that she had fallen so stupidly in love with Leigh
and had allowed this feeling and the dramatic unreality
of their situation to carry her to the ultimate commitment of herself.

'It's probably about time I started getting lunch,' she
said, getting up to go inside. She would eat nothing, she
knew, but the others had to be fed, and she could not let
go now!

Her head and throat were throbbing, and all at once
she was aware that the beat was echoed by a throbbing in
the sky that got louder every minute.

'Listen!' exclaimed Margaret. 'What is it? It's not a
plane, but . . .'

'It's a chopper, it's a chopper!' Lucy and Ross came
screaming through the house, and behind them Nerida
heard Sam start to cry loudly. No wonder! The sound
was so close now that it was quite frightening.

'Is it . . . ? It *must* be coming here,' Margaret whis-
pered. 'It must have seen us. Leigh couldn't possibly
have reached anywhere yet to get help.'

'It's landing!' cried Ross, wildly excited.

Sandy was standing, agitated too. The children tore
around to the back of the house again.

'Don't get too close!' Nerida called after them. She
went through to the back and picked up the sobbing
Sam. 'It's all right, darling. It's all right, love. It's
someone come to take us home.'

She choked on the word and felt faint comfort from

the child's hot little arms around her neck and his little legs dangling around her hip. Even in the midst of the blessed relief of the helicopter's arrival, pain about Leigh still welled inside her, and a child's human warmth and love were good things to assuage it.

In the distance, as Nerida approached, the children waited for the whirling blades to slow and stop, then dashed forward again, and started shouting back.

'It's Jim! Jim's there!'

Nerida increased her own pace. Could that possibly be true? Then she saw Jim Stenning's stocky figure climb carefully from the interior. He looked weak and awkward, and a heavy growth of new red beard was added to his wide moustache. He limped too.

'Jim—you're alive! Oh, thank God!' Nerida was sobbing shamelessly and let her head fall on to his shoulder. He gave her a rough, unsteady pat.

'Takes a fair bit to kill me, mate.'

'What happened?' she demanded.

Lucy and Ross were clustering round now too, wild to hear the story.

'Had to crash-land in the middle of nowhere. Hurt my leg a bit, that was all, but the plane's not in good shape. Knew it was only about thirty miles back here, but couldn't have walked it—just had to wait. Had a few muesli bars and some chocolate in the cabin of the plane. Water lying round in puddles, so I drank that. Caught a rabbit—don't know how I managed that.' He grinned. 'No way to cook it either. Got pretty cold at night. Heard the chopper come over this morning, waved like crazy and I was lucky, they saw me. It was pure chance. We were right, they'd been looking in completely the wrong area. They picked me up and we came straight here. We looked at the old strip as we came over. It's back away there about four hundred yards. It looks quite good. There'll be no trouble getting a plane down on it.'

'Oh, Jim!' exclaimed Nerida thankfully.

'Where's Leigh?' he asked.

The chopper took off again fifteen minutes later with

Margaret and Lucy and Ross. The second RFDS aircraft had already been contacted, and was on its way, expected to arrive in less than an hour. After the chopper had dropped its passengers safely at Benanda, it would return to Jerilda and start to fly over the course of the swollen creek in search of Leigh and his small craft.

In the time that remained before the arrival of the plane, Nerida tidied and organised the old homestead as well as she could, packing up personal belongings and making sure none of the medical equipment was left behind. She even found room for the rest of the bread she had made. No sense in leaving it here to go mouldy and hard, or get nibbled by cats and any mice that had escaped their clutches.

She had just finished doing everything when she heard the thrum of the plane. It was all over, very suddenly. She was returning to the world.

CHAPTER ELEVEN

SYDNEY seemed very cold and cheerless after the bright winter sun of the outback. When Nerida landed at the airport on Tuesday afternoon, low grey rainclouds hung over the city, and it was gusty and bleak. She had been away for less than a week.

'Oh, and by the way, your replacement's arriving this afternoon,' Bill Kirkley, the pilot of the second RFDS aircraft, had announced to her as they flew back to Benanda.

Nerida had given the clearly-expected response of surprised pleasure, but it wasn't sincere. The news meant she would be leaving Benanda within the next couple of days, and, as it happened, it was even sooner than that . . .

Margaret, Sam, Sandy and Joe were all given a night in Benanda's small hospital to check that they had suffered no long-term effects from their time in Jerilda. Nerida doubted that they would. Conditions had been surprisingly comfortable, thanks to Leigh's work and planning, and her own contribution.

She visited each of them in their hospital beds later that afternoon, and felt wrenched when it was time to leave. Sam's Auntie Kath sat at the little boy's bedside, and the two women made each other's acquaintance gladly.

'Annie'll want to thank you,' Kath Thompson said. 'She and the other kids got flood-bound at Jinnalong on their way through. They've been in touch on the transceiver every day and she's been frantic. She knows the good news already, and she'll be that pleased when I tell her how well he's doing. Even his poor little skin could have been so much worse.'

Sam lifted his little arms when Nerida kissed him

goodbye, and again she experienced the bewildering sense of unreality that was almost becoming familiar. Was this little boy really disappearing from her life? Perhaps if she went to see him tomorrow at Kath's, as the older woman had invited her to do, it would only prolong the disturbance to her feelings. Perhaps it was better to say goodbye now, once and for all, and then simply hide in her room at Lorna Hammond's until it was time to leave.

Weakly, she postponed any decision and simply murmured, 'I might see you tomorrow,' as she left Sam's room.

Beneath her concern for the child and the others, too, was a deeper pain that she knew she wasn't even beginning to let herself think of. Leigh. Leigh. Leigh. His name seemed to throb in her very veins. Where was he? There had been no word from the helicopter that he had been found as yet, when the RFDS plane had arrived with them all at Benanda Base.

After she emerged from the hospital, Nerida looked across at the Base building. She could easily go and ask. But somehow she knew she wasn't going to.

'I'm too afraid,' she realised. 'Afraid that if I just mention his name, everyone will know, and will pity me because of Jenny.'

And yet Jenny wasn't coming back. Her new replacement, Sister Lisa Dayman, had already arrived and was at the hotel, temporarily settling in there until Nerida vacated the flat at Mrs Hammond's, and until Jenny's things were packed in boxes and freighted to Brisbane.

Nerida wondered about all this as she walked slowly along the damp red roadside back to Lorna Hammond's. Jenny wasn't coming back. Did that mean Leigh would be leaving too? How would the town react to that news? She had no idea if he was popular here, but felt sure he must be.

'He got thoroughly under my skin in five days,' she thought. 'After two years here, the town is probably eating out of his hand.'

Mrs Hammond had taken time off from her service station to put on the kettle for tea when Nerida arrived back there, although she would go out and serve customers with petrol or snacks if she heard any cars pull in. The older woman wanted to hear all about the past five days, naturally enough, but Nerida had to make an effort to bring out the details of the story. Lorna Hammond sensed this soon enough.

'Have a lie-down,' she advised. 'They've popped the others into hospital, and even given Lucy and Ross a check-over, but no one seems to have thought about you, and you've been through a lot. The responsibility, the uncertainty, the danger—you've handled it all very well.'

Nerida just smiled effortfully and was about to agree that yes, a lie-down was just what she needed, when the phone rang. Electricity suddenly coursed through her. It would be news of Leigh!

But it wasn't. 'You're going out on a plane to Broken Hill at ten tomorrow morning,' Lorna told her. 'And it connects with a flight to Sydney at one-fifteen. That's good news, isn't it? You must be longing to get back. I'll drop you at the Base tomorrow morning. It's a gasfields plane.'

'Yes, that's tremendous,' Nerida nodded without sincerity. She didn't want to leave. But what did she want? There was nothing for her here . . .

No news of Leigh came that night. Was it simply that no one thought to tell her? she wondered at first. But then Lorna rang the Base at half-past nine.

'He hasn't been found yet. There'll be news tomorrow before you get on the plane. Don't worry.'

Has she guessed how important it is to me? Nerida wondered dully.

By bedtime she had a splitting headache and took two tablets before sliding into a hot, heavy slumber that only broke at eight-thirty, when her alarm had been jangling insistently for some time. So she had needed the sleep-in she had allowed for.

It was an effort to drag herself through showering and dressing and breakfast, and she did it all slowly, her head still feeling as if it was stuffed densely with cotton wool, and her limbs aching. Her neck too. She remembered how she had cricked it as she had turned to look for Leigh in yesterday's cold dawn, after their golden passion of the night before. It hurt badly to think of it.

She took her suitcase out the front and put it in Lorna's station wagon, then waited while the older woman served a customer with petrol. Time was getting on. Lorna glanced twice at her watch.

'And there's four jerry-cans in the back too,' the owner of the dirty four-wheel-drive vehicle said just as Nerida thought that they would be off at last.

And so by the time Lorna had closed and locked her service station as well, there was a last-minute race to the airstrip, and Nerida could see that the plane was already waiting for her, its engines roaring.

'But I must find out about Leigh,' she thought wildly. 'I can't leave without knowing. This can't be the end, just like that.'

Lorna said goodbye with a rough pat and some good wishes for the future, then drove off again, reluctant to close her garage for too long in the middle of the morning simply to farewell a comparative stranger. Nerida turned to enter the Base building. Whether the plane was waiting for her or not, she would find out about Leigh. Tears blinded her momentarily, and when she blinked them away the same crewman who had unloaded her baggage from the Tanama plane last Wednesday stood in front of her.

'Got to get going,' he said. 'Here, I'll take the suit-case.'

He swung it into his hand and was already striding towards the plane. Nerida could only follow him. She left Benanda without turning her head back for a last look.

*   *   *

Back in the terrace house at Balmain, Nerida thought she had never felt so desolate, and her jolted and bewildered mind could think of nothing to do, could seize on no activity to occupy her, or pattern to fall into.

'Mum and Dad,' she thought confusedly. 'I must ring them and tell them I'm all right.'

It was eight in the morning in London, and in the background through the surprisingly clear line, she could hear the whistle of their old kettle.

'I'm all right. I'm safe,' she said to her mother.

'What do you mean? Have you had an accident?' was her mother's startled reply.

They had never heard that she was missing in the first place, then. She remembered now that Reid's did not have her parents' phone number, and evidently the matter had not yet become serious enough to attempt to trace them through police enquiries. She managed to explain what had happened and why she had thought it necessary to ring, and then heard some home news. Then she suddenly found herself saying with a sob in her throat, 'I might be coming home soon.'

'Coming home? I thought you were having a wonderful time,' her mother said, sounding worried all at once. 'I was resigning myself to losing you permanently, and having to fly out to visit you every couple of years.'

'Yes . . . Yes, I was having a good time. I am,' Nerida began, gulping back her tears firmly as she started to realise how fraught she must sound. Mum would only be anxious. 'I think I'm just tired,' she said more steadily. 'I'll probably stay on for the year, but not longer. Anyway, I'll write to you, shall I?'

'Yes, do, darling. Travel does make you homesick. We haven't had a letter from you in nearly a month.'

'I know.'

After a few more exchanges they said their goodbyes and Nerida put down the phone.

Genevieve and Susie came home at six and whisked her off to a movie and a Chinese meal in town, wanting to hear 'the whole exciting story'. Nerida told it to them, leaving out anything that was really important.

'And they haven't found Dr Russell yet. You must be dying to know. He sounds quite nice,' Susie said hopefully. She had an eager nose for romance.

'Yes, I would like to know,' Nerida confessed, but kept her voice cool.

'Why don't you ring what's-her-name, Mrs Hammond, and ask?' Genevieve suggested.

It was too late to do so when they got home that night, but she decided to try the next morning. It would be good to know. It would be *very* good to know, even though Leigh's safety could mean nothing in her own life. She was never going to see him again. Time to start saying that to herself now.

'I just wanted to find out if Dr Russell had been found yet,' she said to Lorna, after each had made a few polite enquiries about the other's health and so forth, the next morning.

'Oh yes, yesterday morning,' said Lorna, her voice disguised and faint on the crackly line.

'Is he . . . all right?'

'Well, he's in hospital for the moment . . .'

'Hospital?' echoed Nerida.

'Yes. His hands . . . Look, love . . .' the line was getting worse, 'there's a customer—I'll have to go. Why don't you give me another ring this evening, if you want more news?'

'OK,' said Nerida dully.

''Bye, dear.'

''Bye.'

But Nerida didn't ring again. She had her news. What sense was there in getting more details when she was only trying to forget him?

The days, four of them, passed painfully. On Friday Mrs Reid rang, and when Nerida heard her voice she felt a faint lifting of her spirits. A job, perhaps! Something, at least, to distract her from this awful sense of gloom and dislocation that she didn't have the energy to fight.

But it was only to clear up some details about her pay.

'The cheque from the RFDS has come.' Mrs Reid's voice was clipped and bright as ever. 'We've extracted our percentage and put a cheque for the rest in the post for you. They seem only to have paid you at the standard rate, although I gather you had a rather adventurous time. I thought there might have been a bonus, but no. Their letter did mention that they'd be contacting you directly quite soon, but they didn't say about what.'

The tone implied that Mrs Reid was suspicious about this, and would expect Nerida to supply details as soon as the 'direct contact' came.

'Who . . . was the letter signed by?' Nerida asked weakly. How stupid! Just because she wanted to hear Leigh's name again, and feel she had had some communication from him, even if it was just in the form of an accompanying letter to a cheque. She was acting like an adolescent!

'Dr Ralph Stevens.'

It served her right for being so stupid. Mrs Reid hung up abruptly, leaving Nerida to herself again.

'I must do something!' she thought wildly.

Hadn't she had that feeling before? Yes, it was months ago in England, when she had wanted to run away from the dullness of Damon. Was she going to spend her whole life having to do extravagant things to recover from the effect of men on her existence? The effect of Leigh had been laughably different from the effect of Damon, though.

It was not until Monday that something happened to shake this wild and destructive and miserable mood from her shoulders a little. She received a letter from Benanda—Dr Ralph Stevens again, but its news at least gave her something to think about and plan for.

'In view of your extraordinary response to the unusual and trying conditions you were working under so soon after your arrival, the Kelly and O'Loughlin families have joined with other local people in offering you a token of their deep appreciation . . .' the letter ran. A ticket and brochure were enclosed. They were giving her a week's holiday on the Barrier Reef, starting this Saturday. It was a heartwarming gesture, and Nerida wrote a letter of thanks immediately, clinging to this tiny thread of a link with Benanda and Leigh.

Genevieve and Susie were more excited over this development than they had been over her time at Jerilda. Perhaps that was understandable, since she had said nothing about its real importance to her—Leigh Russell, and her feeling for him that had grown as dramatically and sweepingly as the flood-waters themselves. In any case, their enthusiasm was a positive and infectious thing, and Nerida made herself respond to it.

Under their guidance she acquired a bouncy new bob of a haircut, bought a vibrant swimsuit in tropical colours of turquoise, coral pink, and blue, and a very glamorous black cocktail dress with thin shoulder straps, a figure-enhancing silhouette and a swirl of sequins and beads on the low-cut bodice. She packed make-up, sun-dresses, blouses and jaunty shorts as well, and there *was* a pleasure in thinking about clothes again, after those days spent in one pair of jeans or a white uniform that didn't feel as if it belonged to her.

When Saturday morning came she arrived at Sydney airport again, armed with a new determination overlying the pain inside her.

'I'll at least look as if I'm enjoying myself,' she said to herself as she walked with falsely light step and excited smile along to the airline's departure lounge.

Tangelo Island was a paradise of warmth and colour and life. Arriving mid-afternoon, Nerida unpacked quickly in the cool motel-style room that was part of one of several long bungalows linked by wooden walkways and verandahs set in a lush growth of green, tropical plants and vibrant flowers. It was warm and sunny, and the almost luminescent green water bordered with a slope of squeaky-clean sand looked incredibly inviting.

She spent the rest of the afternoon on the beach,

swimming lazily in the gently undulating water that was protected from waves by the coral reefs that virtually surrounded the island, and then lying on a large fluffy beach towel on the sand, letting the sun lull her into a doze beneath her straw hat, so that she was not thinking of very much at all. She could actually feel knots untying themselves in her limbs and in her stomach, and knew only then how much she had needed this complete escape.

Those few hours on the beach were a strange oasis of peace and tranquillity and contentment, even in the midst of her memories of Leigh which just would not be shut out, and she thought she had made real progress with the long battle of forgetting him.

Thought this until evening came, that was. Then, as darkness folded over the island paradise and she showered away the sea salt that had stiffened on her skin, in the en-suite bathroom adjoining her room, it all came flooding back. This place was just a week in her life. Seven days from now she would be in Sydney again, hoping that Reid's would have found a placement for her.

And it would be . . . what? An average interlude in a private hospital, one of a string that would follow, interspersed with some sightseeing trips around the countryside? Then her year would be up and she would return to London, family, friends, and life on a regular hospital ward.

'But I'm not that person any more,' she realised blankly. 'That's not what I want. I want more adventures . . .'

More tussles with an alien environment, more triumphs as she came to grips with things like wooden dinghies and iron stoves, more of the satisfaction of fear conquered, more glimpses of the power of nature and the beauty of the untamed wilderness, more work with underprivileged children like Joe, perhaps working in other countries too, where poverty and landscape were even starker . . .

And she wanted to experience these things with someone at her side who would encourage her and give her strength, who would challenge her to do things she had not believed she would be able to do, and who would wrap warm arms around her when it all got too much.

She wanted Leigh.

And yet perhaps at this very moment, Leigh was in Brisbane giving Jenny Walters that very support and comfort. Perhaps at this very moment they were in each other's arms.

A crippling, nauseating wave of hurt and envy washed over her, leaving her so weak that she had to lean against the walls of the shower recess to stop herself from falling. Then she was sobbing, her salt tears mingling with the sweet hot water that gushed over her.

For minutes she gave in to it, needing to lose herself in pure, unquestioning pain, but finally she shuddered out a last deep cry and was quiet.

Strength slowly returned. For a moment back there, she had thought she would skip dinner and spend the evening lying on her bed, face down, eyes red and face swollen as she continued to vent her despair, but now she knew she would not.

She would never see Leigh again, but she wasn't going to let this experience go by without learning from it. He had shown her, had called forth from her, resources she hadn't known she possessed before, resources that Damon would not even have recognised or valued, perhaps, and those resources could be used now, too. They weren't only for the desert, for the flood-waters, for Margaret and Joe and Sandy and Sam.

She would dry those eyes, put on careful make-up, blow-wave her new bob, and put on that black cocktail dress, a silver necklace and delicate matching earrings.

She would go out to the open-fronted dining room and eat her meal overlooking the sea. She would chat brightly to the people at her table, whoever they were, finding out about their lives and talking a little about her own. And she would return to her room tonight, late, perhaps after dancing a little, or walking on the beach in bare feet with some new acquaintances, feeling liveable again, at least, if she couldn't feel happy.

'I'm not sure which table I'm at,' she explained to the maître d'hôtel an hour later, pausing at his desk.

He looked up—he was quite young—and gave her an appreciative glance, immediately interested in her plight.

'What is your name, madam, please? I'll just check my list.'

'Nerida Palmer. It should be one of the large tables, I know, the ones for eight people.'

He ran a finger down the list of guests' names. 'No, it's not, actually,' he told her. 'It's table five, for two.'

'I think there must be a mistake——' she began, following him. He was leading the way briskly towards the outside wooden deck at the front of the dining room, where several tables of varying sizes were placed amongst potted tropical plants and flowers. 'You see, I'm by myself here and I specially asked for . . .'

She broke off abruptly. There was a tiny round table in the very corner of the deck, almost hidden by greenery and well out of the way of the traffic of passing diners and waiters. The maître d'hôtel was making his way unmistakably towards it, and as he did so, the man who was unmistakably sitting there, dressed immaculately in a lightweight dark suit and white shirt, looked up from the wine list he was studying.

It was, unmistakably, Leigh.

His smile, when he saw Nerida, was slow and lazy and casual, but his eyes were alight with desire, and she knew suddenly and with absolute certainty that it was going to be all right.

'Leigh!' she exclaimed.

Unobtrusively, and with a faint smile hovering about his lips, the young maître d'hôtel pulled a chair out for her and she slid into it. The dining room was just a haze of lights and laughter and voices. The man in front of her was the only thing that really existed. The contrast between this happiness and her earlier despair was almost more than she could bear.

'My darling Nerida,' Leigh reached a hand across to her, then paused and turned to the waiter. 'Number 15, please, the Veuve Clicquot.'

'Very good, sir.' The maître d'hôtel melted away with a practised flourish.

'Leigh! Your hands!' Only now did Nerida take in the fact that they were bandaged.

'Yes, my love. Do you think I would have left you alone so long otherwise? I've been in hospital. They got very sore and infected after my ridiculous trip in the dinghy. I'm here purely to convalesce.'

'To convalesce . . .' Her face fell. Had she been wrong after all? But he was laughing at her.

'*Purely* to convalesce.' He kissed her own hands, then leant across to her lips and caressed them teasingly with his own so that her doubt melted again.

'And why was your boat trip ridiculous?' she murmured when he released her. Their champagne arrived and she took a bubbly glassful in her hand.

'I simply couldn't trust myself in your company any longer,' Leigh explained. 'I wanted to spend every minute of my time with you, and to tell you all sorts of idiotic things about how I felt. I told myself it was ridiculous after knowing you for . . . what? five days? I knew I couldn't let myself give in to it, when we both had such a responsibility towards Margaret and the others . . . By the way, baby Karen and her mother are both doing very well.'

'Baby Karen . . . You mean . . . ?'

'Yes,' he nodded.

'When?' she asked.

'Three days after you left. Eight days ago, in fact.'

'Then we were very lucky,' Nerida said frankly. 'And so were Margaret and the baby.'

'And it's lucky I kept up the steroid injections—it made a big difference to the development of her lungs. She'll be in a humidicrib for some weeks yet, of course.

Anyway, after . . . that night, I knew it was no good. I was too thoroughly in love with you to maintain my sanity at all, let alone my professionalism. And I was seriously beginning to worry that they'd never find us! The tedious tale of how the mix-up happened in the first place can wait till later.'

'Much later,' she agreed, her eyes shining.

Leigh's bandaged hand was caressing the line of her cheek, and he had leant across to touch her lips again. She drank in the sweet musky male scent that hovered about him and let her slim fingers lace caressingly through his clean, dark hair. People at nearby tables might be watching them, but she didn't care. The waiter might come for their order, but she wasn't hungry yet—or was hungry only for Leigh.

'I was worried—I must tell you this—about Jenny Walters too,' he said after a long time.

'About Jenny?' Her heart turned over for a moment.

'Yes. We'd been going out together a bit before she left,' he frowned. It was a familiar expression, but Nerida could love it now, because she had the right to smooth those lines with words and kisses. 'We got on well enough, but there wasn't much foundation to it. It can happen sometimes in a small town. I realised as soon as she went that I could never feel anything serious for her. But she's a nice girl and I was very afraid that I might have hurt her, and on top of her father's death, that would have been awful. I was mulling over that, and over the disorganisation of the emergency services, the day you arrived, as I watched you walking across from the plane. It got us off on a bad footing, I'm afraid.'

'It sure did!' Nerida agreed fervently. 'It's a miracle we managed to recover from it.'

'I think that says something pretty encouraging about our future, don't you?' Leigh said seriously, his blue eyes fixed on her face in a gaze that was almost a caress. Nerida nodded silently and he brought his head to hers again. 'I dropped in on Jenny in Brisbane,' he went on a moment later. 'She's going to stay with her mother, and it looks as if she and her ex-fiancé are patching things up too, so that's pretty nice.'

'What about your new nurse, Sister Dayman? How's she getting on?' Nerida asked. It seemed funny to think of practical things like the running of the Benanda Base, when she was floating in this heady world of champagne and evening light and Leigh, and it was all she really wanted to give her mind to.

'Darling, she's a disaster!' His laughter was rich and warm. 'She hates it and she's hopeless, and she's handed in her notice already.'

'Then I'll just have to come back myself, won't I?' Nerida said lightly.

'Just don't even try suggesting anything else. We'll spend our week here, doing . . . practically nothing, and then we'll go back together. There's a locum there now, and things have quietened down a lot, but it's still pretty stretched.'

'What do you mean "practically nothing"?' Nerida murmured.

'Or practically everything, depending on how you look at it,' said Leigh, a teasing light of love and desire in his blue eyes.

His lips parted to take hers again in a kiss that held all the promise of what was to come, and Nerida knew that what she felt was a fulfilment that she had not even dreamt of before.

'Do you remember that conversation we had on the verandah of the new homestead at Jerilda?' asked Leigh. 'About great love?'

'Yes.'

'You said it was something that had to be worked on, and I agree . . . but I wonder if we've found ours?'

'I think we've got the right material to work on,' Nerida murmured close into his ear.

They were survivors, both of them... But could they overcome the scars of war?

In post World War One Paris there is a new era, full of hope and determination to build a brilliant future.

Alix Morell is one of the new young women, whose strong will and new-found independence helps her face the challenges ahead.

Jake Sherwood is a Canadian pilot who had fought his way to the top – but whose dreams are shattered in one last cruel moment of war.

Can Alix release Jake from his self-made prison?

Their compelling love story is poignantly portrayed in Ann Hulme's latest bestselling novel.

Published June 1988   **Price £2.95**

W⬤RLDWIDE

Available from Boots, Martins, John Menzies, W H Smith, Woolworths and other paperback stockists